CW01658879

The UNCONVENTIONAL Journey of a Cat Lady

DANI ELIAS

Copyright © 2024 by Dani Elias

All rights reserved. No part of this publication may be reproduced, stored or transmitted in any form or by any means, electronic, mechanical, photocopying, recording, scanning, or otherwise without written permission from the publisher. It is illegal to copy this book, post it to a website, or distribute it by any other means without permission. This novel is entirely a work of fiction. The names, characters and incidents portrayed in it are the work of the author's imagination. Any resemblance to actual persons, living or dead, events or localities is entirely coincidental.

© Copyright Dani Elias. All Rights Reserved.

Copyright Protected with www.ProtectMyWork.com

Editor: Sofia Artola Diaz
Proofreader: Katie Rosenthal

PA Support: Happily Booked PR

Contents

Content Warning

This book includes:

~ Strong language

~ Scenes of sexual nature

~ Adult content

If any of this serves as a trigger for you, please decide if this is the book for you.

If you are sensitive to the description of vomiting, avoid chapter 13!

Finally, the book is set in England and British English spelling is used throughout. That means a lot of times you'll find an "S" where you may expect a "Z". And our ass has an extra Rrrrr to it ;-). Also get ready to learn new words like spotted dick and squirty cream.

Dedication

Between 1980 and 1992, my family and I spent every summer in the north of Italy. Then, in 2018, work took me to Rome, and it immediately elbowed its way to the top of my "Best Cities Ever" list.

So when it became time to send Bri on her road trip, the choice was obvious. Italy was just the perfect setting for a romance full of surprises, detours, and plenty of steam.

To Italy:
Where even cynics start to believe in love!

A special thank you to **Monika Pelizzer** for checking the Italian translations and **Florence** from Happily Booked PR for checking my French!

OUR Roadtrip

The Unconventional Journey of a Cat Lady

UNITED
NGDOM
Little Hadlow
Dover
Calais
Vendeuvre
sur Barse
FRANCE
Salzburg
AUSTR
Milan
Padua
Pisa
Florence
San Marino
Castiglioncello
Grosseto
Perugia
Rome
ITAL

IF YOUR TRIP HAD A FILM, THIS WOULD BE THE THEME SONG

Atemlos durch die Nacht
Helene Fischer

English Songs

- Unbroken – Audiomachine
- Whistle – Flo Rida (in honour of Giovanni #iykyk)
- Without You – David Guetta
- Stronger – Kelly Clarkson
- A Thousand Years – Christina Perri
- Shut up and Drive – Rihanna

French Songs

- C'est la Vie – Khaled

SCAN ME

Italian Songs

- Se bastasse una canzone – Eros Ramazzotti
- Innamorati – Toto Cutugno
- Un'Estate Italiana – Edoardo Bennato & Gianna Nannini
- Più bella cosa – Eros Ramazzotti
- L'italiano – Toto Cutugno
- Insieme:1992 – Toto Cutugno
- Laura non c'è – Nek Filippo Neviani

My photos
Scan me
bitly
explore

The UNCONVENTIONAL *Journey* of a *Cat Lady*

One

The Ex

Bridget

FOLLOWING ANOTHER LOUD BANG Bella has had enough and shoots under my bed. I bend over, holding the girls up. At forty-four my titties are more on the saggy side. I risk blinding myself with a rogue nipple if I bend over without a bra.

"Sorry kitty," I coo and try to give her a gentle pat, but she slides further back under the bed.

"Mum?" Ruthie calls. "I can't find my trainers!"

Did I tell her not to leave packing until the last minute? Yep! Did she listen? Of course not. I thought that at the age of twenty-two my daughter could handle things like shoes. But no, it's still "Mum, where's this?" and "Mum, help me with that."

Christopher's twenty-four and living it up in Japan, teaching English to teenagers who probably behave better than he did at that age. Ruthie, my baby genius, is about to start her Masters in Engineering at the University of Manchester. She's just spent the summer trekking around

South America with her boyfriend, living the dream. Both of my children are responsible adults with their lives mostly together.

Yet the moment they step through the front door it's like they forget how to function. Bella's not impressed either. She glares at them as if to say, 'Mum's mine. Back off.'

I sigh. Maybe it's my fault, I do fuss too much when they're here.

"Muuuuum!" Ruthie shouts again.

"I'm coming!" I holler back. I'll miss her when she's gone but to be honest I'm also looking forward to the sweet sound of silence.

I throw on a T-shirt and open the door to find Ruthie standing in the hallway, giving me *the look*. The one that says I'm the only person who can possibly solve her missing trainers crisis.

"Bold outfit choice," she grins. Fine, the pink T-shirt does clash a little with the bright orange leggings but she was rushing me and that's what was on hand.

"This is my house. I can wear whatever I want." I shrug.

"You could audition for the role of crazy cat lady," she giggles.

"Cheeky. And if I hadn't had to do five loads of washing for you in the last two days because you left it to the last minute, I would have had time to wash my own clothes and dress appropriately."

"I'm shutting up," she mimes zipping her lips.

I open the little storage room under the stairs and find her trainers on the shelf. Just where they'd been the whole time.

"When is your dad picking you up?" My ex-husband reluctantly agreed to take Ruthie to Manchester after moaning again about my not having a driving license because otherwise I could at least have taken her halfway.

William lives still in Hampshire where we grew up and where we lived all our married life. He'd never move anywhere else. I, on the other hand, wanted to get as far as possible away from there after our divorce. My aunty Ruth – Ruthie was named in her honour – was cared for in a nursing home down here in Kent until she passed away four months ago. I loved my aunty Ruth and so I bought a small cottage from the divorce settlement and moved close to her, glad for a chance to spend the little time she had left with her.

"Cuppa?" I ask Ruthie as she follows me into the kitchen.

"No time. Dad will be here in half an hour and I'm still not done."

"Ruthie—"

"I know, I know, you told me to pack sooner but I just wanted to spend more time with you." She picks up a couple of apples from the fruit basket on the kitchen counter and puts them into a shopping bag alongside a bottle of sparkling water.

"You spent half the time you were here talking to Alfie," I retort. She came back from their South America trip two weeks ago and the plan was for us to hang out. I took time off from work and I thought we could do some day trips. We did go to a spa but even there she spent half her time on the phone to her boyfriend.

"I love him, Mum," she gives me a hug. And how can I not be happy for her? They are loved up and when she talks about him I can almost forget my cynicism about relationships. I was like that when I was her age. I got married to William when I was twenty after I fell pregnant with Christopher and back then I actually thought it would last forever.

"I know, darling." I give her a kiss on the cheek just as the doorbell rings.

"Oh no, he's early," Ruthie exclaims, racing off towards her room. She should have known. William is always early – a trait that sadly also applied to the bedroom.

I leisurely make my way to the door, just in time for William to hit the doorbell again. Call it a power play but I don't rush for him anymore.

"Hold your horses," I shout before pulling open the door with a grin. "Hi."

"Bridg," he greats me with a peck on the cheek. His eyes sweep over me but he doesn't comment on my outfit. William liked me to dress "ladylike" when we were married but now that we are divorced he's lost any say in my outfit and he's smart enough not to challenge me.

"It's Bri, like the cheese," I glare at him. No one ever calls me Bridg, but William seems determined to make it a thing because it's the "correct nickname for Bridget." Who makes these rules? In school, I was called Cheesy. Completely my fault, to be fair.

There was another Bridget in class and she'd already claimed Bridg, so I went with Bri, and pronounced it *brie* thinking it sounded exotic but didn't factor in teenage humour. I went around saying, "It's Bri, B.R.I. – like the cheese just without the E." Of course, all my friends heard was cheese, and before I knew it, Cheesy stuck.

"Nav and the boys not here?" I peek past him. We got divorced five years ago and it didn't take him long to date someone new. She was in her mid-twenties back then and I thought William looked like a walking cliché. But against all odds they are still happily married and have two toddlers that keep them busy.

"No, they didn't want to be stuck in the car for even longer. We'll pick them up on the way to Manchester," William tries to push the guilt button as we walk into the kitchen. Do I feel guilty? Not a bit.

"Cuppa?"

"Sure. Why are you not learning to drive? It would make your life so much easier," he asks, leaning against the kitchen cupboards. Ruthie looks a lot like me with her dark blonde hair, grey eyes, and that button nose. But Christopher is the spitting image of William which always hits me when I look at my ex. They share intense brown eyes and wavy dark hair, although William's is showing a lot of grey as of late.

"You know I'm scared of driving." My ability to judge distance and spatial awareness is shit and I never really wanted to learn to drive. "I don't really need a car," I say stubbornly. I mean, that's not completely true. I often wish I could just jump into a car and drive through the countryside because I do miss that freedom driving gives you. But I definitely don't need it for day-to-day life.

William shakes his head. We've had this discussion plenty of times so he knows by now I won't budge and I consider the topic closed. Just as I drop tea bags into the mugs on the counter, Bella struts into the kitchen. When she sees William she freezes, arches her back and hisses.

William automatically moves closer to me and I've to bite my lips. I only adopted Bella after I moved to Kent so she never lived with him but whenever he comes over she makes what she thinks of him very clear. She hates him. I've no idea why because he's never done anything to her. Do I secretly love it? Of course I do.

"Shoo, cat," he whispers and makes a hand movement.

"You're not helping. Just ignore her and she'll ignore you." As if to prove my point, Bella gives him one last nasty look before sprinting out of the kitchen.

William takes the mug from my hand and stirs his tea. He eyes the book I left on the kitchen table.

"Don't tell me you're still reading this... porn."

"It's not porn." I snatch the book from the table and press it protectively to my chest. How dare he talks about my babies like that? I love my smutty romance. I've recently discovered a small-town series set in the Lake District and I'm addicted to it.

"These are unrealistic love stories. Life's not like that," he sneers before taking a sip of his tea.

"Yes, thank you. That became abundantly clear at the end of our marriage." I retort. *I don't get smut shamed in my own house!*

"What? Did I not provide enough kinky sex for you? Well, you never said you were into this shit," he doubles down.

"Any sex would have been a good start," I smirk and know I'm poking the bear here. In general, William and I have a cordial relationship but whenever the conversation falls back to our divorce the knives are out. I can't help but blame him given that he made zero effort to save the marriage and he tends to blame me for not providing what he needed, whatever that was.

"I just didn't feel this anymore," he points between us. I could have bet that this was his next argument.

"Clearly. The only thing I felt in those last years was my own hand." Oh, that arrow hits the target. *I've to stop this.*

"Wait, are you saying you masturbated whilst we were married?" he huffs. *This conversation is getting weird.*

"Of course."

"That's not normal."

"Why?"

"It's weird. Wives don't do that," he says exasperated and with hurt pride.

"Are you telling me you didn't wank whilst we were married?"

"That's not the same."

"What? Why?" I snort.

"Because I'm a man."

"So?" He's really starting to get on my nerves but I'm not willing to back down.

"We have... urges."

"Well, breaking news: women have *urges* too and if we don't get a decent shafting from our husbands, we either have to make do with the two hands the goddess gave us or buy ourselves some decent dildos." I grin. I would have never spoken like this a few years ago but I don't give a shit anymore.

"You're so crude," is the only reply William has. I shrug. I don't care what he thinks of me.

"Daddy," Ruthie slides across the kitchen floor in her socks and gives him a hug.

"Are you ready?" he asks, holding her tight in his arms. William does love our kids, I never doubted that. I just wish he'd spent more time with them when they were growing up. Between work and golfing... opportunities for us to spend some quality time together as a family were far and between.

"Yes, I've put my bags next to the door," she grins.

"I'll load them into the car whilst you say goodbye to your mum." He places a tender kiss on her forehead and leaves us alone.

"I'll miss you so much, Mum!" she whispers and slides her arms around my neck. My throat tightens and I've to fight back tears.

"I'll miss you too, honey. I'm so proud of you." We hug for a long time before she takes a step back.

"Text me when you get there," I ask whilst wiping a tear from her cheek. It doesn't matter how old they get, in my heart my children will always be my babies.

"Will do!" she promises before hugging me again.

It takes them another ten minutes to get all her luggage in William's car and to say goodbye one more time. Eventually William pulls the car onto the road and I watch them drive away until he turns right at the end of the street.

It's quiet when I step back into the cottage. Bella is with me in an instant as I drop onto one of the stairs. She can sense the quietness as well and knows all my attention will be on her again.

"Oh kitty," I cry quietly and scratch her throat. She places her front paws on my thigh and stretches until she can rub her face against mine.

"I love you too," I giggle through my tears. It does hit me hard whenever Ruthie or Christopher leave the house. Although I love the peace, I still sometimes wish I wasn't on my own.

Two

The Letter

Bridget

"Bridget," Ms Elswood pops her head out of her office. She waves me over and I dread to think what she wants now. I work at the PurrInn, an animal luxury hotel. It's a fancy way of describing a cattery with insane features. Cats boarded with us receive only the best cat food, have a TV in their room as well as a tablet, and owners can call them daily. They can also book us to read their feline companion a good night story each evening or order extended one-on-one time with one of the staff members. Of course, all of this costs extra.

"Yes, Ms Elswood?" I join her in her opulent office. She's at least five years younger than me but still insists I call her by her last name.

"Bridget, you didn't read a goodnight story to Captain Whiskers." I want to roll my eyes. That particular cat, with the most ridiculous name ever, sleeps most of the day. He couldn't give a fuck if I read him a story.

"Did he complain?" The minute the words are out, I know I shouldn't have said them.

"No. But I reviewed the CCTV," she snaps. *What the fuck?* That is creepy as hell. "I carry out spot checks, I told you when I hired you. Captain Whiskers' owner paid extra for us to read to the cat."

"I didn't have a chance with Lilo off sick. I'll read him two today," I suggest.

"We provide first class service here and if you're not willing to go the extra mile you might want to reflect on whether this is the right job for you," she dismisses me from her office. *Bitch.*

As predicted, the cat pays no attention to me as I read to him for fifteen minutes before packing up for the day. Maybe I should bring along my smutty romance and read that to the cats. Nobody would hear me except for the furballs and at least I'll get some enjoyment out of it.

Me

The bitch made me read to that snotty cat for 15 min.

I drop a message in our group chat as I get home. If anyone understands my suffering, it's these crazy ladies. Amelia and Miranda have known each other since childhood. I ran into them in a coffee shop earlier this year and we became instant friends. When Amelia rekindled a relationship with her ex, Ben, she introduced us to his sister, Fi, and his business partner's fiancée, Lizzie. And somehow, we all hit it off immediately.

Amelia

Does she actually think the cats listen? Smutty acts like he's royalty, but all he cares about is that he's warm, he's being fed regularly and he gets belly rubs.

Bella weaves between my legs as if to confirm Amelia's point. Yes, she just wants some food.

Me

That's what I said to her. She reminded me that the owner had paid for it so I've to do it regardless.

Fi

I don't know how you keep working there.

I've complained about the job plenty of times but it's so convenient and actually pays very well. Who wouldn't want to get paid to play with cats all day? I was a stay-at-home mum throughout my marriage and when it all ended I applied for just about anything that paid a fairly decent salary. Of course, with my love for art, I bombarded the London museums with my CV, but without any degree or experience, I had no chance. So, in the end it was between the PurrInn and becoming a delivery driver and I certainly prefer dealing with cats to people.

Lizzie

I'm with Fi. Fuck that bitch and get a new job.

Miranda

That. But with less swearing.

Lizzie

:-P

If only it were that easy to get a new job. I'm not even sure if I really want one, and I like working at the PurrInn most of the time.

Me

Are we still up for girls night on Friday?

Lizzie

Abso-fucking-lutely.

Fi

Yes!

Amelia

Of course!

Miranda

Eww, my husband just made me listen to a song about farts. Stay single, Bri! And yes to girls night!

Their replies make me smile. We try to get together as often as we can which between jobs, significant others (aside from me they are all in a relationship) and all the other things life throws at us, isn't anywhere near often enough.

"Right, kitty, how about some dinner?" I get a pitiful meow in return. I think I could feed her a bucket of food every morning and she would still act like she hadn't eaten for days when I get back in the evening.

I'm about to drop my phone on the counter when it rings. I don't recognise the number but my phone doesn't flag it as spam. I hesitate for a second before answering.

"Hello?"

"Good afternoon, Ms Johnson. This is Patrick Pierce, Ruth Wilson's solicitor."

"Oh yes, hi." We'd spoken briefly after the funeral as my aunt appointed him as the executer of her will.

"Ms Johnson, I've carried out all the necessary checks and have completed all the relevant legal steps and can now inform you about your inheritance."

Aunty Ruth had sold her house for a good amount of money before she moved to the nursing home. She hoped it would pay for her care so she wouldn't need to get council support. Her nursing home was lovely but the fees were really high; no way would the council have paid for it. If her money had run out the council would have moved her to a more affordable option. Luckily it didn't come to that.

My aunty was in the nursing home for two years so I don't expect there to be any money left. I'm so glad that she could spend her last years in a comfortable and safe environment that gave her dignity and companionship, I couldn't care less if she didn't leave me anything.

"I can pop into your office on Thursday, if that works for you?" I've the day off and was only planning to do some food shopping as girls night is at mine this week.

"Thursday... I've some time around 11 a.m. Is that convenient?"

"Sure, thank you."

"Great. Have a good evening, Ms Johnson," he ends the call. I was the only one in the family that was very close to Ruth but I expect that she left something in her will to my cousin Bertram. Ruth, my mum, and aunty Janet were close when they were all alive. My mum died of cancer four years ago and aunty Janet, who was the youngest in the group, had a skiing accident when I was in my late twenties. Of the whole extended family only myself and Bertram, Janet's son, are left.

It makes me sad to think there isn't anyone else. I should really stay in touch with Bertram more. But he lives up north so it's not like I can just pop over for a cuppa.

"I know, I know," I reply to Bella's cries as she bumps her head into my leg. "I'm just glad I've you."

I look at the clock for the tenth time. The girls are late and I'm dying for them to get here. My gaze falls back onto the document folder on my kitchen counter. I still can't quite believe the news the solicitor gave me.

When I went to his office yesterday I was expecting to get her lovely necklace with the silver pendant and not much else. I did get the necklace but—

"Finally," I mumble at the knock on the door.

"Come in," I usher Amelia into the house, Fi, Miranda and Lizzie squeeze into the little entrance hall behind her so I can shut the door and keep the cold and rain out. Only once the outer door is closed can we open the one to the living room as otherwise Bella would have bounced and tried to make a break for freedom.

"Oh my god, someone move," Amelia groans as she's squashed against the door frame.

"It's safe to open the door," I call out, leaning against the entrance to the cottage.

They burst into the living room, giggling and laughing, and giving Bella a bit of a scare as she patiently waited for a chance to do a runner.

"Hey, babes," Miranda air kisses me before hanging up her coat in the entrance hall.

"I'm so glad you're all finally here, I've such amazing news," I jump excitedly like a little girl.

"Don't blame us," Amelia objects whilst toeing off her shoes. "This one's like a rabbit," she points at Lizzie.

"Hey, Coop's been away for a whole week golfing in the Lake District, as you well know, since your beloved was with him. Are you telling me you and Ben didn't shag all night?" she challenges Amelia who promptly turns beetroot red.

"None of your business but I was still ready on time."

"What can I say, you have more self-restraint than I do," Lizzie giggles. Fi has disappeared into the kitchen, probably to get some plates for the nibbles they brought with them, but I'm sure the bedroom talk about her little brother was another reason.

"Well, glad you all got shagged but now please sit, sit. I need to tell you my news." I shoo them to the sofa and wait to get their full attention. Lizzie and Amelia argue as always about who gets to sit in the grandfather chair next to the fireplace, which they both love so much. I'm glad to see Amelia win this time because I'm pretty sure last time Lizzie declared it her kingdom for the whole evening.

Miranda rolls her eyes at their shenanigans, directing a grin at me. She doesn't care where she sits as long as she gets a blanket because she's always cold. I know her, so today I've made sure the fire is lit. Still, she drops on the sofa where I left her blanket and tucks her feet under her so she can completely cocoon herself.

"Oh great, and I get the stool again?" Fi groans as she places the tray with plates, mugs, the pot of tea I had prepared and glasses for whatever drinks they girls brought on the table.

"Actually, sit next to Miranda and Lizzie, I take the stool." It's a sturdy poof I normally use to prop up my legs. My living room is small and there is only so much furniture I can fit in.

Lizzie reaches for a piece of cake when I stop her. "No, no food yet. I need your full attention," I giggle excitedly and bounce on the poof.

"Oh my god, what happened? Did you quit your job?" Fi asks as she drops next to the others.

"Not yet," I smirk. There is a small gasp from Miranda and all eyes are on me. "I had a meeting yesterday with my aunty Ruth's solicitor. She left me two hundred," I take a deep breath, "and fifty thousand pounds."

"Holy shit," Lizzie exclaims.

"That's amazing," Amelia chips in.

"You know I didn't expect anything. I was just glad that she had great care at the end. So it all came as a bit of a surprise. And the best thing is that with what I get and what she left my cousin the estate is below the threshold so there is no tax to pay," I clap happily. When I heard the news I was worried the government would be due a chunk of it, but it turns out they won't and it is all mine. Mine!

"Oh my god, what are you going to do with it?" Miranda asks fiddling with the cork on a bottle of Prosecco.

"Give me," Lizzie snatches it from her hand before popping the cork like a pro.

"I don't know. I can definitely resign for now and take some time to look for something better, or maybe I go back to Uni or—" I accept a glass of bubbly from Miranda and gulp down half of it.

"Or what?" Amelia asks.

"I'll get to that. But first, she also left me a letter. Want to hear it?" It's very personal but these four women are like family.

"Sure!" Amelia is quick to reply as she half gets off the chair to grab some crisps from the table. Her left foot remains on the chair to symbolise her claim to said piece of furniture. We are all in our forties but throw us together in a room and you get the crazy attitude of twenty-something carefree girls. The only thing separating us from our younger selves is the knowledge that bending down and picking something up from the floor could be enough strain for our backs to give out.

I pull the folded letter from my pocket, but just thinking about what Ruth has written makes me well up.

"You read it," I hold it out to Lizzie.

Lizzie hesitates for a second but then nods and unfolds the paper.

Dear Bri,

Whenever I say your name, I still see the little girl in front of me that spent hours picking raspberries in my garden. Your hands were pink and so was your mouth as half of the fruit would find its way straight into your tummy.

I never had a chance to have my own children but I always thought of you as a daughter. I was and I am so proud of you. When you were young you had so many dreams and then you fell in love and being a mum and a wife became your new aspiration. I always wondered if one day you would regret not having gone on one of the trips you planned out on the globe in my living room or that you hadn't finished that degree you kept talking about.

Don't get me wrong, I adore Ruthie and Christopher. You're an amazing mum and I don't believe for a second that you regret your time with William even if it didn't end how you had hoped. But now that your children are grown up and following their dreams, maybe it's time to do something for yourself.

I know you, you will spend what I've left to you on sensible things but I beg you to use some of it to go wild for once. Leave your responsibilities behind and have a good time. Explore the world, a new hobby, a new love, but use it to create some memories that you'll look back on in old age with a mischievous laugh. You deserve it and you need it.

I'm just sad that I won't be around to see you travel the globe, to hear the stories of all your adventures and witness a mischievous laugh. You deserve it and you need it.

I'm just sad that I won't be around to see you travel the globe, to hear the stories of all your adventures and witness you glowing with happiness. I've never known anyone who throws herself into everything with so much passion and joy. It broke my heart to see this passion die a little after your divorce.

So, my Bri, go out there, find your passion, fall in love with life and spread your joy. The world will be a better place for it.

Lots of Love
Ruth

Three

The Plan

Bridget

AMELIA DABS THE TEARS away from her eyes.

"That's so sweet," Miranda sighs.

"I know, right?" I wipe my own eyes dry. I've read the letter over and over since the solicitor gave it to me yesterday and I know exactly what crazy thing she wants me to do. But a sense of responsibility is holding me back.

"So, what are you going to spend it on?" Fi asks.

"Don't know," I shrug nonchalantly.

"Yes, you do. You have an idea! It's written all over your face," Lizzie points at me excitedly whilst refilling her Prosecco glass.

"I think we're spending too much time together," I joke but there's no way to hide my idea from the girls. In any case, I'll need their support to think this all through and decide if it's reckless and idiotic or just what Ruth wanted.

"Come on, tell us," Amelia begs and slides onto the floor to sit closer to me. Lizzie uses the moment to steal the chair but Amelia is too excited to notice or react to it.

"I... I always wanted to take a road trip through Italy," I whisper. Silence. Four pairs of eyes are staring at me.

"You don't drive," Lizzie declares. She has always been the pragmatic one of the group; or the one that says it as it is even if you don't really want to hear it.

"I know. But I can hire a driver," I giggle nervously. The fact that they're not immediately excited does raise some doubts in me. "Too crazy?"

"No!" Miranda tries to assure me, "I'm just not sure how happy I am for you to head off into the sunset with a stranger. He could be a serial killer, or something." She shrugs.

I burst out laughing, "I'm not going to hire someone from the street. I'll go through some agency."

"Still," she mumbles. The others are very quiet too.

"You do realise you get into a strangers car every time you call an Uber?" I challenge her.

"Oh, yes, but you don't spend nights with the Uber driver... I hope," Lizzie giggles. *Are they all against it?*

"I won't spend the night with this driver either. We'll have two hotel rooms. I can afford it. I did some rough costings." I was overthinking last night and then started to plan out the whole thing. I hold out a piece of paper to Lizzie where I've dotted down rough numbers based on internet research. With a large amount of contingency and a generous fee for the driver, it should come to around sixty thousand pounds leaving me a healthy amount to make some pragmatic decisions for my future.

"Wow, where did you get all the costs from?" Lizzie asks as she looks down at the list.

Trip Costs

2x Hotel rooms @ approx. £200 a night x 32 Nights = £12.400 Used

Car = £15000 Spending Money £220 per day x 32 days = £8.000

Driver £300 per day x 32 = £9.600

Per diems for Driver £100 x 32 = £3.200

Contingency = £11.800

Total £60.000

"Internet," I shrug.

"Wait, you'll be hiring the driver from the UK?" Fi peeks over Lizzie's shoulder.

"Yes, of course. I want it to be a proper road trip starting right from my doorstep. And it's cheaper if I buy a car and then sell it again. What I'll lose in value is a lot less than hiring a car for a whole month."

"You know what? You need to do this," Miranda says and gives me a hug. "I'm going to be worried, yes. But I can see how much this means to you."

"I... I always wanted to study art history and visiting places like Florence or Rome would be a dream for me. The only holiday William ever took us on was to Benidorm. Not much art there." I take a sip of my Prosecco. "But then I also think it's a lot of money to blow on a trip. I could put it in a savings account—"

"No! You heard Ruth. You need to do something crazy," Fi interrupts me.

"And what about Bella?" When I say her name my little kitty looks up from the window seat where she's lying watching the birds in the garden.

"She can stay with us. Smutty will love it," Amelia claps enthusiastically. Suddenly they all seem to be on board with the idea.

"A minute ago, you all were worried—"

"Yes, but I've a plan," Amelia winks.

"What?" I eye her suspiciously. What could she possibly have cooked up?

"I know a driver for you," she giggles.

"Oh, fucking hell, that's genius!" Lizzie chimes in. Miranda and Fi look as confused as I am.

"Who?" Miranda asks.

"Omar," Lizzie and Amelia say in chorus.

"Who's Omar?" Miranda asks before I can. The fact that she doesn't know confuses me even more. She and Amelia have known each other forever, so he can't be one of their friends.

"Omar is Ben and Coop's company driver," Lizzie smirks.

"They don't really need him anymore but they're hesitant to let him go because he's about to finish his degree and they don't want to leave him in the lurch. He's finished the course and is just waiting for confirmation to come through before he starts looking for a job. He should find out if he's passed before Christmas. It's perfect." Amelia giggles.

"I can't take their driver away." I protest.

"Sure you can. He mainly just sits around. Leave it with us. I'll speak with Ben and Lizzie with Coop and he'll be yours."

"I don't know him." I object.

"Neither do you know any drivers from other companies," Lizzie counters. She's got me there. Why am I fighting this? Oh, I know why. It's the butterflies I suddenly have in my tummy. It no longer is wishful thinking but I'm actually making concrete plans. I want this so much but it's also scary as fuck.

"Well... I can interview him?" I say stubbornly.

"Ha, what are you going to ask him? Can you drive?" Miranda giggles.

"I—"

"No, you're right, you should meet him. Let me speak with Ben and I can set up a meeting for you," Amelia assures me.

"He might not even be interested." I'm planning to be away for a whole month, and frankly, that poor lad has probably better things to do than carting a middle-aged housewife around Tuscany.

"True. But he doesn't seem to have much of a life aside from studying," Lizzie shrugs.

"He's a student. He'll definitely have a busier social life than me," I laugh.

"He's thirty-nine," Amelia says through a mouthful of pizza.

"Now we're talking. Is he hot?" Miranda giggles.

Lizzie fans herself, "Sizzling. Jet black hair, stubble, dark eyes and looks like a movie star in his suits."

"Oh, are you going to make him wear a suit?" Miranda laughs and I can see the word "matchmaking" in all of their eyes.

"Woah, woah. He's going to be my driver and nothing else and I couldn't care less what he wears. Didn't you just all worry about me eloping with some stranger?"

"Yes, but he's not a stranger. We know him, we like him, we approve," Amelia laughs.

"And Ruth said do something crazy," Lizzie protests.

"Yes, but not with the guy I'm stuck with for the whole month. What I want from him is to drive me safely from here to Rome and back. Nothing else." Now, if I happen to run into a nice Italian stallion or two... it's been too long since I've had a dick in me. Why not have a few holiday flings?

Not that I'm going to tell the girls that. If they're worried about stranger danger when it comes to the driver, they'd be even more anxious about my mission to find an Italian stallion to ride. They'd probably send me off with a chastity belt.

"Fine, your loss." Lizzie takes another bite of her pizza.

"All I care is that you're with someone we know and trust," Amelia sighs with relief.

"I haven't said yes yet. Neither have Ben, Cooper or Omar for that matter." Despite my words I doubt there's much chance of Ben or Coop saying no though. They'll do everything for those two ladies. Omar, on the other hand, that poor man might have quite a lot to say to the fact that he's just been volunteered for a month-long shift.

But if he says yes... oh my goodness gracious... I'll be going on a road trip to Italy!

My list of places to visit is getting longer and longer. After the girls left I curled up on my bed and searched the internet for places to stay and see and things to do, Bella stretched out next to me purring like a motor.

I'll miss her and I'm not sure how well she and Smutty will get on. I don't share Amelia's delusion that Smutty will be delighted to have another cat around. Bella and Smutty are both used to being the sole ruler over their kingdom and servants, and it's to be seen whether they're willing to share attention.

At least there are two looking after them. They can divide their attention with one giving Smutty all the loving—probably, Ben who's developed a bromance with that black little furball—and Amelia can look after Bella.

"What do you think, kitty? One month hanging out with Amelia, Ben and Smutty?" I ask. Of course, she doesn't reply; instead, she nips at my fingers, a clear sign that she wants more scratches behind her ear. She loves that.

Both Bella and I jump a little when my phone vibrates with an incoming message.

Amelia

Ben says he'll speak with Omar and if he's interested we can set up your interview.

There are the butterflies again.

Me

Any clue by how much the fee would be?

I based my calculations on some numbers I found on the internet, but Ben will have a better understanding. Amelia's reply is almost instant.

Amelia

Ben said you'll just have to pay his food, accommodation and he suggests £150 per day. That's in addition to his salary which Ben and Coop will continue to pay.

Me

That's not necessary!

Why would they have to pay for it if they're not using him?

Amelia

No, he insists. This'll mean Omar doesn't have to go self-employed and lose out on benefits, pension and national insurance whilst he's with you. Ben thinks Omar's company would charge you an arm and a leg to hire him directly. If Ben keeps him on the books the company wouldn't dare charge them more or cause any issues that Omar travels abroad with you. They can't afford to upset them. So it's easier to keep him on their books and you'll just pay the difference directly to Omar.

Me

That sounds all very complicated.

Amelia

It's not. Just leave it to Ben. All you need to know is that you should offer Omar £150 for the overtime/being available to you 24/7

Me

LOL 24/7, not really

Amelia

Well kind of. You know what I mean. He'll be away from home for a whole month.

Me

Okay. I still think Ben should invoice me for what they are paying to Omar.

Amelia

No way. Consider it a belated birthday present.

Me

You gave me the brunch at the Shard as a birthday present.

They girls were way too generous with their presents but we had such a great day in London when I turned forty-four.

Amelia

This one is from Ben

I shake my head. I know Ben won't blink twice at paying; his and Coop's company is doing very well. So well in fact that both of them basically retired. Nevertheless, it's a generous gesture.

I open a new document on my phone and start noting down interview questions but come up blank. The girls were right, what can you ask a driver really aside from their driving history?

No, there must be more. I'll be spending a lot of time with that guy, I need to somehow make sure we are compatible. What if he likes... Jazz? For some reason that's the only thing that comes to my mind that would be quite off-putting to me. Maybe I'm overthinking this a bit.

Given that he's worked for Ben for quite some time and they all like him, I know he's trustworthy. And surely that's the most important thing.

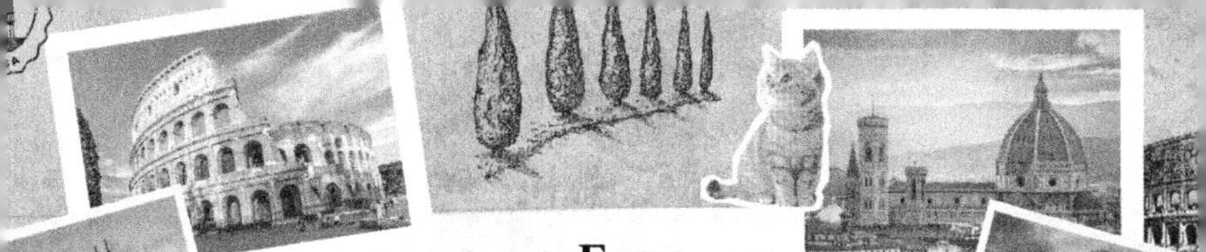

Four

The Relationship-phobe

Omar

THE THUMPING AGAINST MY wall is now constant.

"Jeff, yes, give it to me Jeff!"

Yes, Jeff, for fuck's sake, give it to that guy so he shuts up. My housemate brought home what is the fourth date this week. I couldn't care less how many guys he shags a week, but our walls are thin and there is such thing as too much information when it comes to your housemates.

I grab my headphones and pop them on. I try to focus on my book with the volume yanked up but the relentless beat from my favourite Audiomachine song is in complete contrast to the rather sombre topic of diplomatic negotiations in a conflict zone.

I finally give up and throw the E-reader on my bedside table. I cross my arms behind my head and stare up on the wall opposite my bed. I love the photo I took of the distant summit of Mount Everest framed by trees and prayer flags which hangs on that wall. Seeing Everest from that view-point is one of my favourite travel memories.

My family wasn't too happy when I extended what was supposed to be a gap year into a decade long trip around the world. I've visited most countries in Asia and a fair few in Africa and South America. From shrimp fisher in Vietnam to washing safari jeeps in Kenya, I didn't really care which odd jobs I did as long as it paid enough for me to carry on travelling.

I also spent a couple of years living in Lebanon with relatives of my mum. That had her approval at least, as she was proud that I was willing to learn about the culture she grew up in. I worked in my uncle's hotel and picked up a few useful skills that I was able to utilise to take on seasonal jobs across Europe afterwards. First in Italy, where I combined enjoying the beach and sun with shifts in nightclubs and bars, then I moved on to Austria, where I bartended during ski seasons. Spending the day on the slopes and the evenings mixing Jägerbombs; I had a carefree life with a lot of fun, but no real roots.

Eventually there came a point when my nomad existence was just not enough anymore. There was no life altering event that made me change my attitude. I was just tired. And so I returned to the UK, determined to go back to uni. Most of my jobs abroad included board and accommodation so I actually managed to save some money, not much, but enough to make a start back in England.

I lucked out when Ben and Cooper hired me as a driver. There couldn't be two more generous guys, especially considering they still haven't cancelled the contract even though they really don't need me anymore. Both work part time and rarely late in the evening. However, I have a feeling my luck is running out. They are generous but not stupid, and it makes no sense to keep me on. It's just bad business.

I've interviewed for a few government jobs recently and they've all told me that I'm exactly what they've been looking for, but I need to come back once I have my degree because it's a requirement for the job. So really, I need the job with Ben and Coop for a bit longer. Maybe if I keep very quiet for two months I can fly under the radar and sit out the time until I get my degree. I've used up all my savings—living in London is expensive—and I need the income to pay for my room and potentially a move if a future job requires me to be in a different part of the country.

And I want to find my own place. I'm still house-sharing at thirty-nine and I can't bear it anymore. My housemates are nice but they're all students in their twenties so I don't really have that much in common with them.

Ironically, I'm also the odd one out in my group of friends. Most of the lads are married with kids, living the grown-up life. Sometimes it feels I don't fit in either world.

The music on my phone stops when the phone rings. I take the headphones from my ears and listen. Silence. The porn noises next door have stopped. I guess they're done shagging.

"Hey," I answer Russell's call. He and I play five-a-side on weekends.

"Hey, AWOL." I hate my nickname but I just can't shake it. When I was younger I built a reputation that my numpty friends just can't let go.

"Listen, Lou wants me to invite you over for dinner," Russ says and there is an edge to his voice.

"Is that another matchmaking attempt by your lovely wife?" Somehow I've become the favourite target for my mates' wives when they try to set up their single friends.

The fact that I don't want a relationship is apparently not a good enough excuse.

"Sorry Omar. I tried to talk her out of it," he sighs. I know the guys all live vicariously through me. They love their wives but listening to stories of my dating life has become their new hobby. They're worse than a group of high school girls when it comes to gossip.

"Just tell her I have to work," I chuckle.

"She won't give up that easily," he replies and I know he's right.

"Mate, what can I do to make her stop?"

"Nothing. In her mind you're only single because you haven't met the right person."

Russ might be happily married but I've no delusions about marriage. I've a number of mates who are already on their second or third marriage. A wedding ring does not guarantee a happily-ever-after. My parents are the best example.

I haven't spoken to my father since he walked out on my mum. I was sixteen and the anger sat deep. My mum's family wanted her to move back to Lebanon but she felt at home in the UK and all her friends were here. My brother Stu and I were settled in school and had our friends here too. Moving back was never an option for her.

But I've to give it to our family because they accepted her decision and supported her anyway. My dad never even gave her a penny in child maintenance, so my uncles supported my mum whilst she completed enough courses to find work in HR. Over the years she worked her way up the ladder and when she retired two years ago she'd saved enough alongside her pension to be able to explore the world. I guess I know where I got my travel bug from. Mum and her boyfriend Michael are currently on some cruise in the Caribbean.

Unsurprising my parent's bitter divorce made me a bit of a relationship-phobe. I don't mind dating a woman for a few weeks, but if she starts talking about something more serious I'm out of there. I always set expectations when I start dating them but quite a few have thought they could change my attitude. So as of late, I've stuck to one-night stands. Easier to handle when we both know it's only for one night.

"I'm not interested, so thanks for the invite but I'll pass."

"Great. You know she'll be nagging me all weekend," he sighs dramatically.

"Sorry mate. Can't help you there."

I swing my legs off the bed and head towards the kitchen.

"You owe me a pint after the next game."

"That I'll be happy to provide," I grin before saying goodbye. Crisis averted.

I pull my tie tight as I step out of the house. Luckily my shifts at M&W don't start until the afternoon so when my housemate has late night company, like yesterday, I still have enough time to get a decent amount of sleep before I've to start work.

"Shoo," I try to avoid Mrs Southgate's ginger cat. That cat has got it in for me. Whenever it sees me it rubs up against my legs, leaving cat hair all over my uniform. "Shoo!" I try to scare it away again just as my phone rings. The bloody cat couldn't care less that I don't want to be its friend and purrs loudly as it bumps its head on my leg.

"Hello?" I answer my phone and wedge it between my ear and shoulder whilst digging some ham out of the sandwich in my bag. The moment the ham hits the pavement the cat is all over it. My diversion is a success and I hurry down the path towards the car provided by the chauffeuring service I work for. Sadly, I'm not directly employed by M&W but instead they have hired me and the car through a specialist company.

"Walter, it's Paul." Of course it's Paul. My boss is the only one in the world who calls me Walter.

"Hey."

"Listen, I want to give you a heads up. I don't think M&W will renew the contract with us for a second driver."

I lean back in the driver's seat and take a deep breath. Although I had been expecting the news it still hits me hard.

"I'm afraid I've no other account at the moment for you so when they confirm that they only need one driver I'll have to let you go." Now I feel sick. This means I'll have to look for a new job just for a few months. If I had my own car I could maybe be an Uber driver, but I don't, nor do I have the savings to buy one.

"Are you sure there isn't anything else? Isn't there usually more demand before Christmas because of all the Christmas parties?" I suggest, although I'm not hopeful.

"Sorry. We've already taken on some temp drivers," he dashes my hopes.

"Okay, thanks for the heads up." There is no point in pleading, clearly he's made up his mind.

"Sorry." He says again before hanging up. *Well shit. I guess I'll spend the evening hunting for a job.*

Five

The Proposal

Omar

THE ORCHID ON THE reception desk has twenty leaves. I've counted them twice, that's how bored I am. I've been waiting in Ben and Cooper's office for nearly forty minutes.

When I came on duty at three, I was told to report upstairs rather than go and take over from the other driver.

I know what this is about and I wish they'd just get it over and done with. I appreciate their decency to tell me themselves but it doesn't change anything on the outcome. I'll be without a job soon and then I'll have to make some tough decisions on what next. I could maybe move in with my mum for a few months, but the thought of asking my mother, as a thirty-nine-year-old man, if I can stay with her and her boyfriend fills me with dread. Of course, I can apply for other jobs but the companies looking for someone at short notice don't usually pay very well and rent in London is high; even if you're sharing. Isn't selling photos of feet on Only Fans a thing? But I doubt my hairy Hobbit toes will appeal to anyone.

"Omar, sorry to have kept you waiting." Ben drops a folder on Gladys' desk.

"No problem, Sir." I know he hates being called that but one of my colleagues once used the client's first name because they'd asked him to. Our boss overheard and fired him as soon as he could. This has become company folklore, and every new driver hears about it on their first day.

"Come on in." He points to the open door of his office with a sweeping motion and lets me step in first before closing the door behind us. I've only been in here once before which was on my first day when I was introduced to Ben. Since then I've always waited in the staff canteen or in my car. Ben's secretary Gladys, or someone else from the reception team would call me whenever I was needed.

There's always a lot of waiting around during the late shift, especially after all the staff have left. In the past, I would wait around to take Ben home. Lately, though, there's been even more time spent doing nothing. Ben and Coop are now both in relationships that keep them at home more than at the office. Occasionally, they take their significant others out for dinner and avoid the hassle of trying to find parking by asking me to take them. Aside from that, there isn't usually much else to do anymore. Before I finished my degree, I used that time to get some coursework down. Now, I usually just end up doomscrolling through my phone.

"Please, have a seat." Ben straightens his tie as he drops into his office chair. I almost grin because I know he hates the tie. It's the first thing he takes off the minute he gets into my car and he always lets out a sigh as if he can finally breathe again.

There's silence in the room. Ben looks uncomfortable and doesn't seem to know how to start.

"Sir, I don't think this conversation is necessary," I try to make it easier on him. "Paul, I mean Mr Blake, called me to let me know." Ben gives me a curious look.

"And what would it be that Paul told you?" The mischievous glint in his eyes makes me wonder if maybe I've got this wrong.

"He… he called and said you won't be extending the contract for a second driver."

"Not true. Not sure where he got that from but I'll get Gladys to call him. Coop and I've agreed to keep you on until your degree comes through. And if you need references for any jobs you plan to apply for please give them our details directly."

"Oh. Thank you. That's very generous of you. I… I'd understand if you had to let me go though. It's not a good business decision and—"

"Omar, you've shown complete dedication and loyalty to our organisation. We live in a time when even an NDA doesn't stop staff gossiping if the price is right. It would be a bad business decision to repay your commitment to this company for the last three years by dropping you so close to you achieving your goal. We pride ourselves on being fair employers and this is only fair."

I'm not sure many company owners out there would agree with their decision but Ben and Coop have always operated differently to others. There is a persistent rumour making the rounds that they cancelled an important business contract because the manager of the other company insulted Ben's girlfriend, Amelia. I don't know if it's true but I can definitely see him doing that for Amelia.

"Actually, what I need to ask you is a bit... strange. How would you feel about a road trip?"

I relax at those words. Next week he and his girlfriend are going to Yorkshire for three months. To be honest this is why I thought he would be letting me go now. Once he's up north the company definitely doesn't need a second driver.

"Of course, I can drive you and Ms Foley to Yorkshire." Not sure why the song and dance about it. It's a five-hour drive, so not really a big deal.

"No. That's not what I meant." Ben leans forward. "Amelia's friend Bridget is planning a road trip from Kent to Rome and back. She can't drive and so she's looking for a driver. Amelia and I would feel more comfortable if the person joining her is someone we know and trust. But I do realise this is outside your normal remit and would come with a substantial time commitment. M&W would continue to pay your salary and Bridget would pay for the overtime, accommodation and per diem."

I'm not sure what to say. I expected to get fired and instead he's offering to pay me to gallivant around Italy.

Ben folds his hands in front of him. "Let me assure you that we'll absolutely understand if you're not interested and it wouldn't change my promise that we'll keep you on until your degree comes through."

"I... no, of course I can do that. When would the trip be?"

"November."

"November," I repeat. *Who goes to Italy in November?*

"Yes, Bri needs to finalise some things here first. If you're interested she'd like to interview you, which I guess is understandable. We were thinking maybe tomorrow afternoon. But if you want to think about it first—"

"No, that sounds very interesting. Tomorrow afternoon is good." I reply quickly. Ben sighs with relief and types something on his phone before putting it screen up on his desk.

"The only thing I'd suggest is that you let me handle this with your boss. As he's already told you he'll let you go, I'll ask him to let us employ you directly; that way we don't need any discussions about you working abroad. You will receive your salary directly from us from now on and Bri will pay you an additional hundred and fifty pounds a day." I do some quick maths in my head. I can sublet my room for a month so the rent is covered, I'll have accommodation and food paid for and I get extra salary. I guess luck is with me after all.

"I don't know what to say, Sir."

"No, no, if you're employed at M&W you have to call me Ben." He points at me with a cheeky grin.

"Ben," I nod. "I'll make sure your friend has a safe trip around Italy."

"I don't doubt you will." The screen of his phone lights up and a small smile appears on his face as he reads the message. "Amelia has arranged your interview... audition, call it what you want, for tomorrow afternoon at three at the coffee shop near my house. You know where that is?" he asks.

I nod. I spent a lot of evenings studying in there—luckily that place is open late—whenever Ben needed me to wait before taking one of his dates home. But that was way before he met Amelia.

"I'll be there. And, thank you. I know you don't have to do this," I tell him with honest gratitude.

"On the contrary. You're doing me, and Coop, a favour because if you hadn't agreed Amelia and Lizzie would have worried the whole time that Bri's away." We shake hands before I leave. I feel like a ton of bricks has been lifted from my shoulders.

My Italian might be a bit rusty but it's still good enough to get around. This could actually be an awesome month of travelling through Bella Italia and gorging on pasta, and to top it off I'll get paid to do it. That's as close to a jackpot I'll ever get. One last adventure before I take on some desk job. All I need to do now is convince the woman that I'm the man for the job. *Piece of cake!*

I park the car in a side street not far from Little Hadlow's village green. I've pictured myself living somewhere like this more than once when I've driven through to drop Ben off. I've had enough of London and the overpriced rental market. Given that I want to work in government diplomatic services I'll probably never completely get away from city life but a rural and cosy place like Little Hadlow, within commuter distance to central London, that's where I see my future.

As I round the corner, I spot through the big front windows that the coffee shop is not busy at all. It's a weekday and the after-school invasion hasn't hit yet.

The warmth of the coffee shop is a welcome relief from the cold and misty October day. I rub my hands together to warm my fingers as I approach the counter to order a coffee. Casually scanning the room, my eyes land on a woman in the furthest corner. She's tapping the wooden table with her fingers whilst scrolling on the phone in her other hand. She matches the description Ben texted me: a short, blonde woman in her forties with a cat handbag. I thought the description was a bit vague, but Ben had shared my company photo with her so if I can't find her, surely she'll recognise me.

I glance at the woman again as the barista slides my coffee across the counter. I can't tell if she's short and I definitely won't guess her age, but she has a cat handbag and nobody else in here does. *Here goes nothing.*

As I approach, I can see her giggling at something on her phone. Her face lights up and makes her look way younger than forty something. *Maybe I do have the wrong woman?*

"Ms Johnson?" I ask cautiously.

Her eyes find mine and a big smile spreads across her face. A warm smile, a welcoming smile… a cute smile.

"Omar! It's so nice to meet you," she jumps up and moves towards me like she wants to hug me before catching herself and holding out her hand stiffly. A rose tint appears on her cheeks.

"Nice to meet you." I grip her tiny hand and squeeze it. Standing in front of me, it becomes apparent just how short she is. I'm not the tallest guy ever at five-foot-eleven—I certainly don't match the six-foot something tall, dark and handsome description that every thirst trap online comes with—but she can't be much more than five-foot-four.

We take a seat and I slide the print out in my hand across the table.

"Oh, yes, your CV," she picks it up and starts to study it. "I would have offered you a coffee but I can see you—" She stops herself and looks at me over the top of the paper. "Your name is Walter Omar Brown?"

"Yes."

"Ben always called you Omar."

"Yes, that's my middle name. I don't like Walter." She studies me briefly before nodding to accept my very vague explanation.

"AWOL!" a voice shouts from behind me.

Fantastic!

Six

The Interview

Bridget

Oh wow. When Omar's eyes find me, I forget to breathe for a second. He looks a bit like Haaz Sleiman. *Okay. Put the brakes on and send your hormones on a hike, because what he looks like is neither here nor there.*

I drop my gaze back to the CV just as a loud male voice echoes through the coffee shop.

"AWOL!" Omar flinches as a man in his early forties slaps him on the back. "What are you doing out here?"

"I'm—"

"Hi, I'm Bri," I hold out my hand to the stranger.

"Russell. I'm AWOL's friend." He gives me a friendly smile.

"AWOL?" *How many names does this man have?*

"Yes, it's a nickname," Omar says through clenched teeth.

"But your name is Walter Omar Brown. Shouldn't it be WOB?" Russell lets out a deep belly laugh and slaps

Omar, who looks like he'd like to murder his friend, on the shoulder again.

"I like her," Russell gives me his seal of approval. "We call him AWOL because when we were younger he had a habit of slipping out of the ladies' bedrooms in the middle of the night."

"Oh." I don't know what else to say. I'm pretty sure Omar didn't expect his interview to go like this.

"But I don't think he does that anymore and he would be silly to do it to you," Russel grins at me.

"Russ—"

"Thank you, I guess," I interrupt Omar, "but we're not on a date. This is an interview. A job interview," I clarify. That wipes the smirk of Russell's face.

"Oh... shit. I'm sorry, AWOL... Omar... mate, I'm sorry. I'll leave you to it. Nice to meet you. Oh, and he's a very responsible guy." He gives me an embarrassed wave.

"Except when it comes to the ladies?" I can't stop myself from smirking at both of them. Russell gives me one last awkward grin before heading to the counter to pick up two coffees to go.

"I apologise for my friend," Omar mumbles. *God, does he always talk like he's the Prime Minister's butler?*

"Don't worry, AWOL." I just can't help myself. His sheepish look is just too cute. Purely in an eye-candy kind of way, of course. Thinking about it, I should keep my distance because with those dimples, dark eyes and general yumminess he might scare away potential holiday flings if they think I am with him. Not even this thirst trap of a man can keep me away from my mission of getting some dick aka *Operation Mount the Italian Stallion*

"So, tell me about yourself?" Omar seems to relax a little when I make it clear that this whole interlude with his friend hasn't ruled him out of the job. He rattles off his credentials just as listed on his CV and then looks at me expectantly.

"Thanks for repeating your CV." I can't help but giggle. "But if you come with me on that road trip, we'll be spending a lot of time together. It would be good to know what kind of person you are."

"I am professional, hardworking, discreet—"

"Do you drive well?"

"I... I follow road traffic rules and I don't have any points on my license."

"No, are you a stop and speed driver?" He stares at me unsure what to say. "You know, someone who drives and breaks, drives and breaks." My words don't seem to have cleared anything up, going by the look on his face.

"I'm not sure I understand."

I blow out in frustration. "Well, there are the drivers that look ahead for obstacles and slowly reduce speed as they approach and then there are those that keep the speed and then break quite hard and abruptly." I mime the motion.

"Oh, I'm definitely not a... stop and speed driver," he grins. Flippin' heck, his whole face transforms when he doesn't frown. It makes his eyes sparkle. *Maybe my mission should be to make him smile more?*

"Oh good. It makes me feel queasy and we don't want me to vomit all the way to Italy," I giggle. When I see the horrified look on his face I quickly add, "But don't worry, I don't tend to get travel sick." He just nods. "What music do you like?"

"What music do I like?" he asks. I'm not sure why he's baffled by every question I ask him.

"Yes. Music. I want to make sure we're compatible."

"It's not really a concern what music I like. I will listen to anything you want." He gives me another look making it clear he thinks I'm a bit nuts.

"You might regret saying that," I laugh. I'm taking his words as a challenge to see if I can find music that will get him to drop his weird subservient demeaner.

"Do you like cats?" This is a key question.

"Is a cat coming on the trip with us?" He eyes me suspiciously.

"No. It will just tell me a lot about your character." Aka if you're one of these militant dog people who think that all cats are evil, I don't want you in my car.

"I don't have a cat." We are eying each other like two Cowboys at a high noon duel.

"That's not answering my question."

"I don't have strong feelings about them either way," Omar replies diplomatically. So not a cat person but not a cat hater either. I guess I can live with that.

"Okay. Well—" I've run out of questions to ask. I already knew that he's probably not a psycho killer, so I should just offer him the job.

"Can I ask you a question?" He fiddles with his coffee cup.

"Sure."

"Why do you want to take a road trip in winter to Italy? Most people go there for the sunshine and a trip to the beach."

"I don't like heat. I sweat like a snowman in a sauna." That makes Omar laugh out loud. Yes, laughing definitely suits him better than his serious demeanour. "No, but seriously. I'm not much of a beach person. I want to soak up the culture, visit museums. Who wants to do that in thirty degree heat? And at the end of the trip, we'll drive through some places that are supposed to have lovely Christmas markets. That's way more up my alley," I shrug.

"Which kind of brings me to the next question…. what's the plan? Ben just said one month road trip through Italy." He takes a sip from his coffee.

"Right, so this is what I'm thinking…" I pull out my folder and show him my rough plan:

1. 31 Oct Little Hadlow to France
2. 01 Nov France to Milan
3. Milan: 2 or 3 days
4. Pisa: 2 days
5. Florence: 3-4 days
6. Rome: 4 - 5 days
7. Perugia: 4 nights
8. San Marino: 3-4 days
9. Verona: 1 Day
10. Padua: 2 days
11. Salzburg: 3 days

2 Spare Days - Return to UK on 30 Nov

"We should stop somewhere in France on the way to Milan, but I'm not sure where and I didn't allocate days to any place because I want the flexibility to decide how long we stay in each place. But I need to be back in the UK on the first of December. My son is getting married."

Christopher called me yesterday with the news that he'd married his Japanese girlfriend. They eloped with just their best friends as witnesses. And now they are planning small celebrations in the UK and Japan for their family and friends in each country. Sadly, the only time they could get off to come all the way to the UK was at the beginning of December so that has kind of put a firm return date onto my trip.

"I've a cousin in Vendeuvre-sur-Barse. I know the village quite well and that would be a good stop-over point." Omar types something on his phone and then turns it around to show me the location on a map.

"That sounds great! Have you been to any of these other places before?" Amelia mentioned that Omar travelled when he was younger.

"Yes, I worked in Italy for a year or so. Rome, Florence, and I worked in Rimini, which is not far from San Marino. I also worked in ski resorts in Tyrol in Austria for a while. So I speak fairly decent Italian and German and I'm fluent in French and Arabic."

If we were in a cartoon my jaw would drop.

"You speak four languages?"

"Well, five," he laughs, "if you count English. My mum is originally from Lebanon so I lived there for a few years. That's where I picked up my Arabic and French. And then, as I said, I worked in Italy and Austria. I've an ear for languages and always found it easy," he shrugs like it's not a big deal.

As a person who, in typical English fashion, reverts to shouting when abroad, in the assumption that makes it easier for people to understand me, I'm mighty impressed. Could he be any more perfect for this job?

"Okay, last question, and this is the clincher," I wink at him, "are you planning to wear that for the whole trip." He looks down at his perfect dark suite and purple tie.

"This? That's my uniform," he replies with affront in his voice like I asked him to strip here and now.

"I know but I'd feel like I'm the star in Driving Miss Daisy. And I'm not *that* old," I giggle.

He locks eyes with me and I forget to breathe for a second. *Jeez, maybe I shouldn't hire him. I might run the risk of suffocating.*

"What would you like me to wear?" It's a simple question but somehow it feels loaded. All sorts of images pop into my head. Images that have absolutely no business to be in my head. Like him in tight black boxer briefs. *Holy cannoli woman, get a grip. I'm randier than a teenage boy seeing a Playboy magazine for the first time. Do they still print them? Argh, focus.*

"Something more casual," I say and take a sip from my water. My throat is dry, must be the warm air in here.

"You're the boss." He smirks at me and I'm wondering if my horniness is written all over my face. To distract myself, I hand him another piece of paper with all the terms. Day rate, per diems, anything else I'm paying for. He scans over it and just nods.

"Great. So do you want to think about the offer? As far as I'm concerned, the job's yours if you want it." *I'm going to Italy, I'm going to Italy.*

"No, this all sounds good to me." He pulls a pen from his inside jacket pocket and signs underneath my signature on the sheet of paper with the terms before pushing it back to me.

"Okay, great. I'll email you a copy. Wait until you meet the Beast."

"The Beast?" Omar looks puzzled again.

"The Mercedes I bought for the trip. It's a GLA or something but it has a lot of boot space." I was delighted when I got a good deal at the local dealer.

"You bought a car?"

"Yes?"

"Alone?"

"Yes?"

"You bought a car with nobody advising you?"

"Why? You think I need a strapping lad to make sure me little woman buys a decent car?"

"No. I think you need someone who understands cars, who can check it's in a good condition. What's the milage?" Oh, he looks grumpy again.

"I don't know. It's German," I blurt out. I mean, everyone knows they make the best cars, right?

"So?"

"German cars are reliable, everyone knows that." For a brief second there is an amused smirk on his face then he's serious again.

"I suggest I pick up the car this week and give it a once over. And you should get a mechanic to look at it."

"The car salesperson said the Beast is in good shape," I protest again, but even I know that's not really a strong argument. The car dealer is hardly going to tell me that the car is shit, is he now?

"I'm sure he did." Omar shakes his head and pulls the piece of paper he signed earlier back to his side of the table. For a second, I'm wondering if he's withdrawing from the job but then he jots down his phone number on the top of the document.

"Text me when it's a good day for you and I'll come to your house and get the car." At some point during the conversation he dropped his subservient demeanour and now he's a right-bossy-boots. And I like it. No, I don't like it, my vajayjay likes it.

"Yes, Sir," I mock salute him and he squints at me again like he's wondering what he's gotten himself into, but then lets it go. We agree that I'll email him the agenda I have so far so he can research the route, and then we say goodbye for the day.

When I get back home Bella is already pacing like a caged tiger, desperate for her dinner and some belly rubs. I get this little pain in my stomach when I look at her. One month without my snugglebug will be tough... but it's just a month.

As Bella's loud smacking noises fill the silence I lean against the counter.

"I'm going on a road trip through Italy," I whisper each word slowly just to allow myself to actually believe it. *Thank you, Ruth!*

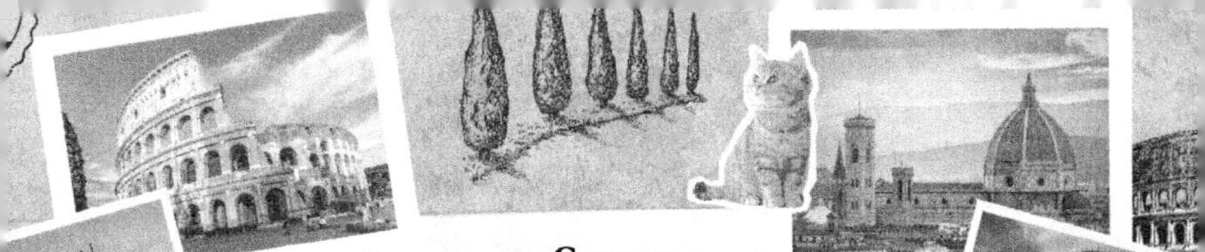

Seven

Le début

The Beginning

Omar

MY NECK FEELS STIFF from sleeping on the sofa for the last two nights. I found a nice couple to rent my room but they needed it from last Saturday and that meant I had to camp out in our living room. Not ideal, but the prospect of staying in comfy hotel rooms for the next month made it all worth it.

The train is slowly creeping towards Little Hadlow. I left my house just before five and I feel tired already, but I promised Bri – she keeps insisting that I call her by her nickname—I'd be there by six for an early start. *Nothing a strong cup of coffee can't cure.*

I've spent the last two weeks trying to get things fixed on the Beast. I'm not sure what it is, but she's in love with that stupid car and refused to exchange it for one with better milage and in better condition. Her argument that it's German doesn't make up for the fact that the last owner must have done the Rally Dakar or something with it because it was in a dire state. Between me and a mechanic mate of mine though, I think we got it travel ready.

My efforts earned me a tight hug from Bri. That hug has stuck with me, its warmth lingering like a ghost. And that citrusy scent, fresh and vivid, has slipped into more than a few of my dreams these past nights. Dreams that were highly inappropriate.

"Next stop: Little Hadlow." The automated announcement pulls me from my thoughts. I gather up my oversized duffel bag and small backpack and head to the door as the train slows down.

A thin mist hangs over the village, creating a fitting atmosphere given that it's Halloween today. I walk the short distance to Bri's house in the darkness. As I approach I can see Bri busy hauling a large suitcase through the front door. She places it next to the car where there are already a number of other suitcases and bags.

"What's this? You're bringing all of this?" I ask.

"No. I thought I'll introduce all my bags to the Beast and find out who wants to come with us," she smirks before adding, "Morning to you too."

"Morning. And what are all these?" I point at the bags again. There's enough luggage here for a small family.

"We are going for a month and a woman needs choices," she giggles. I'm not quite sure how I'm going to fit all of these bags into the boot. It's a big boot, but—I guess it's a good thing that I packed light.

It takes about fifteen minutes of playing suitcase Tetris before we got it all stowed.

"Oh, I forgot something," Bri gasps before running back into the house. She returns with a large cooler and a see-through plastic box filled with what looks like a ton of crisps and sweets. She puts both on the backseat with a grin.

"What's a road trip without snacks?" she giggles. I just shake my head. All I need is a coffee, and pronto.

"Are we ready? What about your cat?" When I picked up the car to get it checked out she insisted on introducing me to Bella. To Bri's delight and my dismay, the tabby cat immediately rubbed up against my legs and purred.

"Lizzie and Coop picked her up on Friday to take her up north to Amelia and Ben," she replies with a little sadness in her voice. I feel I should say something to bring her smile back but I'm not sure what.

"Are these prawn flavoured crisps?" I ask, eyeing the snacks on the backseat.

"Yes!" She perks up instantly, as if I've just reminded her the world still has some magic left.

"Great, but don't get too excited," I say, grinning. "You're not eating those in the car."

"What? Why?" She puts her hands on either side of her hips looking at me sternly like a head mistress. A sexy head mistress. *Mind out of the gutter, Omar!*

"Because they stink."

"How dare you! Is it too late to ask for a different driver?" she asks with mock exasperation in her voice.

"I'm afraid so," I chuckle.

"Fine," she shrugs and her eyes crinkle as she holds back a laugh.

"Alright then. Let's go," I announce causing Bri to squeal with happiness.

"Wait, departure selfie!" She grabs my upper arm and pulls me close. *There's that citrusy smell again.*

"Smile!" she demands before taking a selfie of us with the Beast in the background.

Excitement radiates off her. The closer we got to the departure date the more she bombarded me with messages about things we can do and things she wants to see. She followed each of the messages with an apology explaining that I don't need to join her on any sightseeing tours if I don't want to… unless I want to.

A few times I wondered if there isn't anyone else for her to talk to about this trip. I know Ben and Amelia left a few weeks ago for Yorkshire, but I'm sure she's still in touch with them on a regular basis. Nevertheless, I seem to have become her go-to person to discuss our journey. I don't really mind. Actually her enthusiasm is contagious and made me start to look forward to the adventure more and more.

I connect my phone to the car and open the satnav. We are heading to Dover first to hop on a boat to Calais. It's quite straight forward to get there but I always like to have the satnav ticking along to warn me about traffic.

"OK, right. Let me set out some rules." Bri turns to me from the passenger seat

"You're making the rules?" I ask.

"It's my trip. I make the rules," Bri replies. "Rule number one: we only listen to local radio stations."

I drop the hand that was about to press the start button for the car. "Why would that be?"

"I want to fully immerse myself in the culture of the countries we're travelling through, and music is part of it."

It's clear from the expression on her face that this is not up for discussion.

"OK, fine. But you do realise that the majority of the songs they listen to will be similar to the UK?" There's no escaping Swift and others, regardless of where you go in Europe.

"Rule number two..." She completely ignores my counterargument. "... we have to have a comfort break every two hours. I need snacks on a regular basis. And I've a bladder the size of a pea."

Now that's a rule I won't argue with. "Works for me. I need coffee." Bri nods before holding up three fingers.

"Rule number three. I need to be near Wi-Fi every evening at four on the dot."

I study her and wait for more details.

"Why exactly?" I ask when she doesn't elaborate.

"Because I've arranged with Amelia that I'll call Bella."

"You're calling your cat?"

"Yes. Why is that crazy?"

"Because it's a cat. What are you going to tell her? She's not going to know what's happening. Are you expecting her to report back about her day as well?" Maybe I shouldn't mock her, but this is a bit silly.

"Don't be stupid," Bri mumbles embarrassed and blushes. "I just want to see her."

"Every day."

"Every day."

"OK, your trip, your rules. What if there's no Wi-Fi?"

"There has to be Wi-Fi. Every petrol station has got Wi-Fi nowadays. Four o'clock, cat talk."

"Four o'clock, cat talk," I repeat and finally press the start button.

"Rule number four..." Bri continues. Apparently we're not done with the rules. "... you tell me when you're tired and we stop. No questions asked."

"Happy with that but I can usually go for quite a long time."

"That's what he said," Bri giggles.

"Sorry?"

"Nothing. And rule number five... I can't think of a rule number five. Well, actually, I do know a fifth rule. No farting in the car."

I laugh out loud. I can't help myself.

"You do realise I'm doing a job here? I know how to behave professionally." I side-eye her. There's a smug grin on her face. She's teasing me, the little minx.

"Well, I'm just putting it out there. Don't get too comfortable, Mister."

What have I let myself in for? I indicate to join the road towards Dover. Traffic is light, which I take as a good omen for the start of our trip.

"OK. Do you have any rules aside from banning prawn cocktail crisps?" Bri asks.

"I thought your trip, your rules?"

"Well, you might have something you'd like me to do." For a split second, my mind wanders somewhere wildly inappropriate. *Fuck.*

"OK, rule number one: if you feel queasy or travel sick please tell me. I can stop at any time. I prefer that to having to clean the car." I glance at her and she's nodding.

"I can agree to that."

"That's the only rule I have." Really, I'm quite easy going.

"Well that's an easy one, I would have done that anyway. Liking that outfit, by the way." Her voice is laced with humour.

"You asked me not to wear a suit," I protest. To be honest, I'm quite glad that she made that request. Wearing a suit from morning to evening would have made for a long month. Instead, I'm in jeans and a T-Shirt.

"I know. I was just complementing you." She smirks with a mischievous look in her eyes that I can't read "Our ferry reservation is for eight thirty. We should make that, right?" she asks when I don't reply.

Bri hasn't really prebooked much. So far, she's only reserved the boat to Calais and the hotel in Milan for two nights, as we know when we'll get there. From then onwards we'll take it day-by-day to allow us to stay in some places longer if she loves it there or leave others sooner if we run out of things to see.

I've spoken with my cousin Khalid in Vendeuvre-sur-Barse and we can stay at his. He's got a large farm on the outskirts of the village and plenty of space for guests. Bri fought me at first because she felt she was imposing, but she doesn't know my family. Welcoming guests is in our Lebanese blood. You arrive as a stranger but you leave as an adopted member of the family.

The journey to Dover was quick because this time of the year there aren't that many people travelling down South. Bri just stared out the window with a happy smile on her face, singing along to the radio. She's got a beautiful voice, I've to give her that.

Once we've crossed the channel, she started a new game of making me pronounce the name of every city and village on the motorway signs.

When she wasn't testing my French, she was either pointing out all the little things she spotted that are different from home or scanning through the radio channels until she found one with French pop music. Her head bobbed along and she mouthed some sounds, even if she couldn't pronounce the words or understand what they actually meant.

I'm mesmerized by her. She is showing the joy of a young teenager exploring the world for the first time. And it makes me wonder why she's never done this kind of travelling before.

"Can I ask you something?"

"Sure."

"Did you and your husband never take a trip abroad?" In one of our meetings about the trip she let it slip that she's divorced.

"Why do you ask?" She doesn't seem to be offended by my question, just curious.

"You take it all in, like every little thing matters, even if all we've seen so far are just endless French fields."

"My husband preferred tradition and continuity. Every year we'd fly to the same holiday resort in Benidorm. But the last time we went the hotel had closed down and he had a major meltdown. We ended up at a different place and he spent two weeks complaining about how everything was worse than at the other hotel. Don't get me wrong, Benidorm is alright, but I've always wanted to go on a cultural trip. I wanted to study art history; I've always been interested in art. I dreamed of going to Rome, Paris, and Vienna to see beautiful works of great artists. But my husband wasn't into that, and with two little children the last thing you want to do is drag them through museums while they scream and shout. I wouldn't have enjoyed it."

"I get that."

"But now I've got a chance to see it all!"

"Yes, you do," I agree, noticing the big smile on her face. I can't help feeling sad that she missed out on her dreams before, but I'm happy I can help her fulfil them now. I've never held back for anyone. I've always done what I wanted, explored the world, and saw the places I wanted to see. I don't know what it's like to put your wishes behind someone else's, and I admire her for that. I promise myself I'll make sure this trip is everything she hopes for.

Today's drive is rather mundane. The French countryside here isn't exactly thrilling. Just endless green fields stretching on and on, broken up now and then by a sleepy little village. The motorway feels deserted, with hardly a lorry in sight. Most of the freight traffic sticks to routes through Brussels and Germany to dodge the tolls, so we're making steady progress without any trouble.

We've stopped twice so far to stretch our legs and grab a coffee for me and more snacks for Bri. I don't know where she puts them all. She's been munching on bits from her box throughout the journey and every time we stop she orders herself another croissant. I can't help but smile when she declares the most recent one the best one so far, just as she did with the previous one.

Bri holds out her bag of snacks to me and this time I can't resist. I take one of the sweets and slip it into my mouth.

"Thank God, I thought you're a non-snacker... one of these health freaks," she laughs.

"I do try to eat healthy," I reply. "But you found my Achilles heel." I point at the bag of Colin the Caterpillar sweets.

"Good to know," she smiles. "So, tell me, what are you going to do once you get your degree?"

"I was thinking of getting a job with the Foreign Office or something. I've applied for a few jobs but they all need me to have my degree confirmed first. So, I'm waiting it out."

"Sounds interesting. And with your languages you should have an advantage," she says before stuffing another sweet in her mouth.

"True. However, I'm also considering working for a charity. Sometimes I wonder if that's the better way to go. Governments are driven by politics, not necessarily by what is right or fair. And I wonder if a charity would just suit me better." Truth be told, I'm feeling quite uneasy at the moment about working for the government because there are many things about current policy that I don't agree with and that's not going to be beneficial for a career at the Foreign Office.

"That makes sense. You should speak to Amelia. She worked for a charity."

I don't reply. I'm suddenly aware that we're only a few hours into the trip and it already feels nothing like a professional relationship. Bri, with her bubbly persona and relaxed attitude, has made me feel like a friend. Yes, this feels more like two friends on a trip together. And I like that. I like that a lot and that worries me a little. I've been hired for a job here; Ben trusts me. I mustn't lose sight of that.

Eight

Les Français

The French

Bridget

Alright, so I know driving on the French motorway isn't exactly the highlight of our trip. But honestly, I'm loving it. Everything looks just that little bit different from back home—villages, churches, you name it. I'm soaking it all in and tucking it away in the memory bank.

Every time we pull up at a petrol station we're greeted with a cheery "Bonjour!" I reckon that's the only French word I've truly mastered. Well, that and "croissant," naturally. And "merci," of course. So, yeah, I'm basically a pro at ordering my favourite pastry by now. "Bonjour. Un croissant, s'il vous plaît." Omar can't help but laugh every time I march into a petrol station, brimming with confidence, ready to dazzle them with my tiny French vocabulary. Luckily he's there to translate when the conversation goes beyond baked goods.

I think I've had three croissants already today and a ton of snacks. I'm going to return from this trip three stone heavier. Do I care? No! I'm going to enjoy this trip, diet be damned. Besides, I'll be doing a lot of walking through museums and looking for sights. That'll burn off some of the croissants.

Omar is pretty quiet unless I nudge him into a chat. He doesn't say much, but I reckon that's just who he is—probably used to it from work. Still, I've made it my mission to crack that shell of his. We've got a whole month together, and I want to know the real Omar, not just the guy who loves a bite of Colin the Caterpillar.

The only thing I know for sure is that Omar thinks I'm a bit bonkers. We stopped at a motorway services and I decided it was the perfect time to ring Bella. Omar sat there, watching me with an amused look on his face, like he wasn't sure if he should laugh or not. Every now and then I'd catch him biting his lip, trying to keep a straight face while I babbled away to my snugglebug.

I tried to explain why I call Bella every day (aka, pull some ridiculously scientific bollocks out of my arse to cover the fact that I just miss her), but he just raised his hands and said "No judgment," before going quiet again.

It wasn't like I was saying anything weird—just the usual, "Are you being a good girl? Have you eaten your food? Do you miss me?" But apparently that's not what normal people do at a service station. As I'm mid-conversation with Bella an old French guy strolled past, looking thoroughly confused. He pointed at me and said something in French.

Omar grinned and replied. Whatever he said included the French word for cat, so I can guess what this convo was about. The French bloke's eyes practically popped out of his head. He muttered a very dramatic "Mon dieu!" and shuffled off like he'd just witnessed a three headed dog. And of course he returned to his family sitting nearby who were soon having a good look at me like I was their entertainment for the afternoon.

When we pass the first sign for Vendeuvre-sur-Barse I notice a tiny smile on Omar's face. I wasn't sure about staying at his family's place at first, but he made a good point. Why hole up in some boring motorway hotel when we can enjoy a bit of his family's hospitality? And now seeing that smile, I get it—it's not just about convenience.

I've brought along two bottles of wine as a thank you and I've made Omar promise to tell me if there's anything else I can do to pitch in.

Omar turns off the radio as we pull into the courtyard of a sprawling farmhouse. A door swings open before the car comes to a complete stop and out charges an older lady, about my height, waving her hands excitedly. She's quickly followed by what seems like half the village. Just how big is Omar's family?

"That's my cousin's grandmother-in-law, Aurélie, but we all see her as our grandmother." Omar says before exiting the car.

As soon as he's out, she's got him in a bear hug, which is no small feat considering he's got at least seven inches on her. She's chattering away in French, hugging and kissing him on the cheek between every other word. Omar just laughs and tries to keep up with her questions. Hearing him speak French does things to me; I want to fan myself. This man needs to stop getting hotter by the minute.

I hang back a bit, unsure what to do with myself. It's a bit awkward, barging in on such a lovely family reunion. Omar's passed around like a beloved teddy bear, everyone giving him hugs and kisses.

I briefly consider grabbing my bag. I've packed smartly, with a smaller suitcase holding everything I need for tonight, saving us from having to schlepp all the luggage in. But before I can get to it the old lady spots me, shouts "Bonsoir!" and makes a beeline straight for me. Next thing I know, I'm wrapped in her arms too.

She smells of lavender and something sweet, like cake. It reminds me a little of hugging my aunty Ruth because she also always smelled of lavender.

I smile politely and reply with a masterful "*Bonsoir*" which she takes as an invitation to let off a stream of French. Omar interrupts her to explain that I don't understand a word she's saying. She just smiles, pats my cheek and then waves us into the house.

Omar tries to introduce me to the rest of his relatives but there are so many names I'm not sure I'll remember them all.

"And this is my aunt Thérésa," Omar guides me to a woman in her sixties. "She's my mum's sister. They both left Lebanon around the same time. My mum settled in the UK and my aunt in France."

"It's nice to meet you," I say and hold out my hand in greeting.

"Nice to meet you too," Thérésa replies with a strong accent before gently swatting my hand away and pulling me into a hug. "Now come, come, dinner is ready." She ushers us into the house.

Omar puts a hand on my back just below the shoulder blade and guides me towards the entrance. "Should we get our suitcases?" I ask nervously, trying to avoid going into the house. I'm still feeling a little awkward that I'm invading someone else's house and interrupting what could be a lovely family meal.

"Nah, leave it to me. I'll get them after dinner because the food is probably already on the table waiting for us, and you don't want it to get cold. Her cooking is amazing."

He leads us down a long hallway into a large kitchen with a massive oak dining table. There are more new faces waiting for us and Omar is pulled into hugs and kisses again before we finally all end up around the table laden with food; food I've never seen before, but food that smells delicious.

I sit between Omar and his cousin Khalid who speaks English. He keeps pointing out dishes and explaining if they are Arabic or French.

"My mother likes to mix both cultures. I guess in modern cooking it's called fusion," Khalid chuckles. I like him. There's a tiny bit of resemblance to Omar, but his nose is bigger and his eyebrows bushier. His skin looks withered. And his smile is crooked with slightly tinted teeth, probably from smoking.

Most men around the table, except for Omar, seem to smoke. Except when it's time to eat. Aurélie shouts at them like they're little boys and they all obediently get rid of their cigarettes.

By the time the meal is done, I'm stuffed. Omar's whole family made sure I tried every single dish and took seconds and thirds. Whilst I was feasting, Omar kept chatting up a storm with his family. I haven't seen him as lively or happy... ever. Okay I don't know him that well yet but seeing him with his family makes me even more determined to succeed with my mission of making him smile more.

I think his aunty Thérésa caught me watching him; she gave me a wink and a knowing smile that immediately made me blush. *Great, now his family thinks I'm a cougar trying to shag the young man in my employ. Only, he's not that young, really. He's only four years younger than me and—okay, I need to fucking stop this train of thought because...no!*

"*Bridget, es-tu mariée?*" Aurélie asks, her eyes twinkling with mischief.

"She's asking if you're married," Khalid translates with a grin.

"Divorced," I reply with a casual shrug, trying to play it cool.

"*Pas de petit ami?*" she presses on after Khalid relays my answer. And just like that, everyone's eyes are on me. Including Omar's. Do I have a boyfriend, Khalid passes her question on to me.

"*Non,*" I say, leaning on one of the few French words I've got up my sleeve.

"*Omar est célibataire aussi—*" Aurélie's grin widens.

"*Grand-maman!*" Omar cuts her off, clearly mortified.

"What did she say?" I ask, curious and slightly amused.

"Nothing," Omar mutters, but his vague response makes everyone else at the table burst into giggles.

"She said Omar is single too," Khalid chuckles, earning himself an evil look from Omar.

"Just ignore them," Omar mumbles, looking thoroughly embarrassed as he grabs his plate and heads to the sink. "They've got a habit of trying to marry everyone off." His move seems to cue the others to start clearing the table, and I'm secretly relieved the spotlight is off us.

Sure, Omar is fan-yourself hot, but I don't think my cynical take on long-term relationships would go down too well with this crowd of happily hitched couples.

After dinner Omar and his cousins head outside to play football, leaving me with his aunt and the other women. We don't say much, just sit there smiling and watching the lads kick the ball around. It's comfortable now, not awkward at all. They've really made me feel at home and I'm glad we decided to stay here. Maybe we could even pop in again on the way back to England. *Yeah, I'd like that.*

I can't help but admire Omar a little as I watch him running around with his cousins. Alright, maybe more than a little. There's something about the way he moves—so confident, so effortlessly cool. And then there's that smile of his, the one that lights up his whole face and makes you forget your own name for a second. I'm putting this down to my general state of perpetual horny-ness and the fact that it has been a long time since a man has paid me as much attention as Omar. Even if I obviously pay him for it. This just is all so wrong. I need to get him out of my head and focus on the stallions that await me when we finally get to Italy.

As Omar kicks the ball towards the goal, narrowly missing, I let out a small cheer. Omar's eyes land on me and he gives me a big grin that definitely makes my body forget the agreement we just made about focusing on Italian stallions. His aunty throws another knowing look at me, so I mumble an excuse and head back into the house. I need a cold shower.

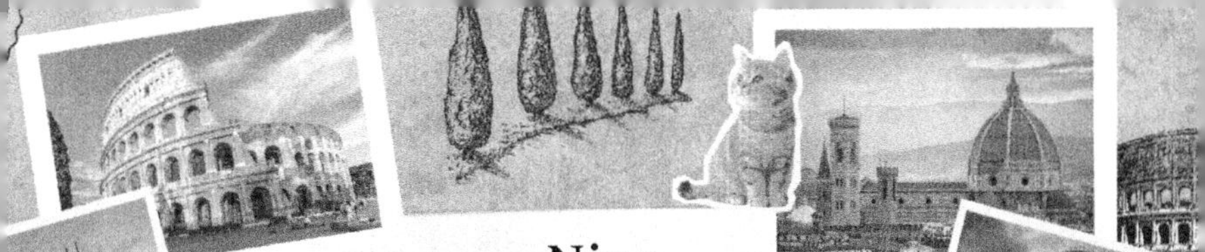

Nine

Il momento illuminante

The Lightbulb Moment

Omar

I CAN'T HELP BUT grin when Bri cheers from the sidelines. Naturally, my family all start giving me knowing looks and I shake my head, trying to send them a silent message to cut it out. The last thing I want is for Bri to feel awkward.

We keep playing for another half-hour until we've had enough. By the time we finally call it quits, my T-shirt's practically glued to me, and sweat's dripping from my hair.

"Alright, spill—what's really going on between you and Bri?" Khalid asks as we cool down by the small fountain in the farm's courtyard. He loves practising his Arabic with me so when we're alone that's the language we switch to.

"Nothing," I say, a bit too quickly.

"Come on," he laughs, "you couldn't take your eyes off her at dinner."

"Don't be ridiculous. I was just making sure she was alright," I reply with a frown. *Did I really look at her that much? I didn't think I had.* Sure, she was adorable when she blushed after Aurélie asked if she's single, but other than that—

"Omar, it's me. You can tell me the truth," he presses, dropping onto the bench next to the fountain.

"I'm serious. It's purely business," I insist, digging my heels in.

Khalid studies me for a moment, then hits me with, "What if it wasn't just business?"

Bloody hell, that's a loaded question.

"I... you know I don't do relationships," I mutter.

Khalid lets out an exasperated sigh. "Oh my god, are you still on about that? Look, what happened between your mum and dad was rough—he was a right arsehole, and your mum's better off without him. But come on, look at the rest of us. We're all happily married. I'd die for my wife. Not every relationship has to end in complete disaster."

I shrug, knowing he's right but not quite ready to admit it.

"Don't you ever feel lonely?" Khalid's family to me. We got tight during our time in Lebanon, even with both of us already having siblings we care about. I know whatever I say will stay between us. But am I ready to admit it? I don't even like admitting it to myself.

"Doesn't mean I have to jump on my boss," I sigh, half-admitting the truth.

"What if she wasn't your boss?"

"I wouldn't be here," I chuckle, trying to deflect.

"No, don't play dumb. You know what I mean. If you met her somewhere else, through friends or something, are you really telling me you wouldn't be interested?"

"I don't know," I mumble.

"Yes, you do," he shoots back, calling me out.

"Fine, what do you want me to say? That she's beautiful? That her joy for life makes me want to show her the whole world? That I can't stop smiling when she orders another croissant in her adorable Frenglish—" *Okay, where the fuck has this come from?*

Khalid just grins. "Now that you've admitted it to yourself, what are you going to do about it?"

"Nothing."

"Nothing?"

"Nothing," I repeat, resolutely. "She's my boss."

"That's a shit excuse. Firstly, plenty of people fall in love while working together. And second—"

"Whoa, whoa, who said anything about falling in love?" I object quickly.

"And secondly," he continues, ignoring me, "I'm not talking about a casual fling. We're talking about you having real feelings for her, and her having real feelings for you—"

"She doesn't," I interrupt.

"You're starting to piss me off," Khalid says, shaking his head. "Fine, spend the whole trip driving around Italy pretending you're not attracted to each other. But I'm telling you now, it's going to be a long month." With that, he stands up and heads towards the house, just as Bri steps outside.

She's wearing my hoodie, the one I left inside, and she's got a sheepish grin on her face.

"Sorry," she says, tugging on the fabric, "I couldn't find the car key to get my bag and I was getting cold." She drops down on the bench next to me. The moon's up now and the night is clear. Our breath forms little puffy clouds in the chilly air.

I know I should probably get out of my sweaty clothes before I catch a cold, but with Bri sitting next to me, I'm suddenly not in any rush to move.

"Sorry, I should've grabbed your suitcase before the game," I say.

"Don't worry," she replies, gently touching my upper arm. "Your family's great."

"They are," I grin, feeling warmth that has nothing to do with the leftover heat from running around and everything to do with her hand on my arm.

"Thank you for bringing me here. It's the perfect start to our trip." She flashes me another big smile. Our trip. Again, it almost sounds like we're friends on an adventure together, not just me doing a job.

"You're welcome." We sit there in silence for a little while.

"So how come your mum moved to England and not here with her sister? If you don't mind me asking?" She looks at me with the same curious eyes that she has every time when she reads yet another interesting fact about Italy from one of her guidebooks.

"During the civil war in the seventies and eighties a lot of young people tried to leave Lebanon. My mum got a job as an au-pair in London. My aunt moved to France to marry my uncle, who she was engaged with before he left for France to study here."

"Oh, that's romantic."

"Yeah," snort. "More romantic than my mum's story. She fell in love with a British man, they married and had two boys and that's when my dad realised maybe having a family wasn't for him, so he buggered off." I sound bitter.

"Oh. I'm sorry. Is your mum still in England?" Her hand is on my arm again.

"Yes. She had friends there and me and my brother had never lived anywhere else so she stayed. But she always made sure that me and my brother know where we come from. We both have a double name representing England and Lebanon. His is Stuart Khalid and mine is Walter Omar. I just always hated Walter because I felt it made me sound like an old man and so I've gone by Omar ever since I can remember. Stu goes by his English name."

"WOB," she giggles and I can't help from grinning myself.

"Mum's on a cruise in the Caribbean at the moment with her boyfriend." She didn't ask so I'm not sure why I'm telling her.

"I'm glad she found her happy ending," Bri says.

"Yeah." We both stare into the distance, lost in our own thoughts, until Bri breaks the silence again.

"Omar?"

"Yes?"

"Can I tell you something, as a friend?" Bri asks with a serious look on her face. Knots are forming in my tummy and my heart starts racing.

"Sure." My voice is almost a whisper.

"You really need to take a shower," she laughs and then pulls the collar of my hoody over her nose pretending I stink to high heaven.

"Oh, funny," I chuckle and poke her in her side, making her squeal with laughter.

"Don't! I'm really ticklish," she giggles.

"Fine. I'll go and get our suitcases and then will take a shower so *madame* doesn't have to put up with my B.O. any longer." I get off the bench and head towards the house to grab the keys from where I left them in the kitchen.

"I'll wait here in the *fresh* air," Bri calls out after me. I shake my head laughing. *What can I say to that?*

Khalid's words are swirling around in my head as I step into the shower. There's no denying Bri is a stunning woman, anyone with eyes can see that. But she's more than just a pretty face. She's feisty, sassy, warm, and has a sense of humour that could brighten up even the dullest moment. It's no wonder she's managed to charm my entire family. They've all, in their own not-so-subtle ways, dropped hints that they'd love to see me as something more than just her driver.

Of course, these are the same people who think marriage is the answer to everything. *What do they know?* When I got back into the house I found a few texts from Mum that made it obvious Aunt Thérésa's been gossiping about me and Bri. Apparently, the family grapevine is running overtime and now half of them are convinced I'm secretly smitten with Bri.

I'm relieved we're leaving tomorrow. Once we're back on the road I can put this matchmaking nonsense behind me and focus on maintaining a professional relationship. But, if I'm being honest there's a nagging voice in the back of my mind telling me I'm deluding myself.

———— ♥ ————

We've been stuck in this fucking traffic jam for nearly two hours now and we've barely moved. It's driving me mad. There has been a massive pile-up ahead of us and now everything's come to a standstill.

Bri's mood doesn't seem to be affected. She just sits there bobbing along to French pop, not a care in the world. I, on the other hand, can't stand it. It's painful. And not just metaphorically. I need to piss so badly.

The brake lights on the car in front of me dim and it rolls away. But not for long. He comes to a stop again after a metre at most. I follow him slowly as we sneak our way along the motorway. After about 30 minutes I finally see an exit. There's no point staying in this nightmare.

"I think we're going to turn off here," I tell Bri, drawing her attention on me.

"Do you think that's wise? The surrounding roads will be gridlocked as well."

"If we cut to the east and drive along the German border we can bypass this whole section. It might be a little bit longer distance wise but, given that nothing is moving here, I'm sure it'll be faster. I scan the map on my phone and there are no traffic jams indicated on the route to the east.

"OK, sounds good," Bri grins. I don't know if anything ever shakes this woman, she just takes it all in her stride.

A few other cars have the same idea and the exit is busy as well, but once we get past the first roundabout we're on a quiet road. Most of the cars were just trying to bypass the one junction, but we are heading away from it all together and that means the roads are clearing quickly. As we get closer to German border the radio station loses reception and white noise fills the car instead. So Bri is back on her mission, trying to find the next station to listen to. She comes across a German one. This close to the border airwaves crossover and you can pick up both countries' signals.

"Ohh, this sounds amazing!" Bri hums along to a song that was a huge hit in Germany a few years ago.

"Can you translate the song for me?"

"It's basically about living in the moment and experiencing the thrill of love and freedom, as a couple races through the night, feeling invincible and lost in passion."

"What's it called?"

"'*Atemlos durch die Nacht*'. That means breathless through the night."

"Oh, I like that! I need to add this." She pulls out her phone and starts typing.

"What are you doing?"

"I'm compiling a list of songs I like and that can become my playlist when I'm back home to remember this trip." She smiles. Her happiness is so infectious.

"How do you spell the title?"

"A.T.E.M.L.O.S. New word D.U.R.C.H new word. D .I.E. New word N.A.C.H.T."

She finishes typing and then tries to pronounce it. I have to bite my lip. It's not bad for a first try but it's still not even close.

"It's *Atemlos durch die Nacht*." I try to pronounce each word clearly. Bri repeats it again and she's getting better.

"What's the artist called?"

"Helene Fischer," I reply.

"How do you know so much about it?"

I shrug. "It just was a very popular song in German speaking countries a few years back when I was living in Austria. Everyone knew this song and they played it over and over during après ski."

Bri gives me a big smile and returns to bobbing along to the music. It's a cheesy love song but if it makes her happy, who am I to judge?

A few hours later we pass the border sign indicating that we are now entering Italy. Bri claps excitedly.

"We're here. We're here, we're here," she shouts.

"Just about," I reply, but I can't hold back a grin. Again, her joy is so infectious. "Right. How about a first cappuccino? I know it's not that far to Milan but I could do with a coffee," I suggest.

"A break sounds great. I can call Bella. Oh wait, I thought Italians only drink cappuccino for breakfast?" she asks, holding up the guidebook she always has to hand.

"I'm not Italian," I wink at her.

"Well, if you would like to be authentic you should drink espresso," she points at a page in her book.

I crinkle my nose in disgust, "No disrespect to Italians, but I need milk in my coffee."

"Typical tourist," she giggles and jumps from the car. I can't wait to point out that her beloved croissant, which she'll be scoffing down any minute now, is even less authentic than a cappuccino. Two can play this game!

Ten

Il gigolò

The Gigolo

Omar

I HAVE NO IDEA what she thinks she's achieving with these calls to her cat. She spent a solid ten minutes giving Bella a blow-by-blow account of last night's dinner, while the furball just sat staring out the window, clearly not bothered. Bri was about to wrap things up when a black cat suddenly ambushed Bella and all hell broke loose.

The tablet went flying, Bri was screaming, Amelia was shouting through the tablet, the cats were screeching, and then—*boom*! The video cut out. Pure chaos. It took me five minutes to calm Bri down, and even then she didn't really settle until Amelia rang her back to confirm that the two little warriors had been put in separate rooms for a time-out. Honestly, cats are mad.

Amelia kept reassuring Bri that Bella and the other cat, Smutty, usually got along before I managed to get her back in the car so we could finally continue our journey.

I'm exhausted by the time we get to Milan. These have been two long days of driving, especially with the time wasted in the traffic jam. The new route took us through Switzerland and when we got close to some of the highest peaks of the alps Bri's eyes filled with so much amazement that I took her up the St. Gotthard Pass rather than taking the much quicker tunnel under the alps. There was already snow on top of the pass but thanks to the warm sun we were able to have lunch on the terrace of a hotel next to one of the small lakes dotted around the pass.

It's only because we had a booking for a hotel in Milan that we eventually moved on rather than spending a night up there. The view was amazing and I'm sure Bri would have loved watching the sun set.

Our unplanned trip in the alps meant that we arrived in Milan well past sunset. After settling into our hotel not far from Milano Centrale—I have to show Bri the food market there before we leave—we decided to head out again for something to eat. The young receptionist in our hotel gave us a tip for an authentic restaurant frequented by locals which sounds a lot better to me than one of the more prominent tourist hot spots.

The waiter greets us with an enthusiastic, "*Buonasera. Benvenuti nel nostro ristorante.*"

He seats us at what he describes as the best table in the house but I can guarantee he says that about all of his tables. I thank him as he hands us the menus and ask him for some water. Out of the corner of my eye I see Bri hanging on every word I say. She looks mighty impressed every time I speak a different language and I've a hard time not to let this get to my head.

"Oh my god, this all sounds delicious. I can't decide," Bri groans. In the end she's torn between the Carbonara and the Lasagne so I offer we order both and swap half way through. She loves the idea and seeing the joyful smile on her face was worth the suggestion. Every time she smiles at me like this I feel a pulling in my guts. Some romance authors would call it butterflies but I'm calling it a bad idea. Nevertheless, I seem to go out of my way to do or say things that make her give me this smile.

She looks around the room after the waiter has taken our order.

"I can't believe we're here," she says and for the first time since my conversation with Khalid yesterday, I look at her differently and not just as a paying passenger.

I hold up my glass and say "*Benvenuta in Italia*!" Bri clinks her glass with mine.

During dinner Bri entertains me with stories about her children and I laugh because they sound oddly familiar.

"Reminds me a lot of what happens when me and my brother visit my mum."

"You also turn into small children?" she smirks.

"I'm nearly forty, but of course, I still let my mum spoil me," I object.

"So it's the mother's fault."

"Well—" I laugh whilst Bri feigns indignation and throws a piece of bread at me.

"Who's the child now?" I ask, picking up the piece of bread from where it landed on the table and putting it in my mouth. All I get in reply is a big smile. The one that causes the knots.

Of course, we can't resist tiramisu for dessert and it's then that I notice Bri keeps looking behind me. I'm about to turn to see what is going on when she stops me.

"Don't! Don't turn around. There is a man who keeps smiling at me," she explains lowering her voice.

I don't need to see the guy to know he's a wanker. Anyone who flirts with a woman who's with another man is a bit of a knobhead. There was nothing in mine and Bri's interaction to indicate that we're not a couple. Actually if anything, it was a tad flirty, so what he's doing is rude. But I don't say anything. It's not my place.

"I think if you were to leave he'd come over and make a move," she giggles like I'm one of her girlfriends. A new feeling is filling my guts and I swear it's jealousy and maybe also a bit of disappointment that she can push me aside so easily.

"Do you want me to leave?" My voice sounds cold even though I'm trying to be casual.

"Is that rude? I'm rude. I'm really sorry. It's just... I've got a secret kind of mission to have a little bit of *fun* and this Italian stallion looks like fun." Her cheeks turn pink with embarrassment. She looks adorable when she blushes. "You're judging me," she whispers.

"I'm not." Not sure if my protest holds up though. My voice gives me away.

"Yes, you're. And I think that's not okay from a guy who's called AWOL." She crosses her arms in front of her defiantly.

"I haven't said a word. I've not judged you."

"Yes, you have. Why is it that it's okay for man to go on holidays and have a fling or two, but when you do it as a woman it's wrong?"

"It's not wrong. I just didn't think you'd be that kind of woman." *Uh oh, I'm digging my hole deeper.*

"What kind of woman would that be?"

Yup, I had that coming.

"I don't know. Don't listen to me. Let me go back to the hotel room and give you a chance with your Italian stallion. Just promise me you will stay safe. And text me if he gives you any problems."

Not sure how I feel about leaving her here with this knobhead. Ben and Amelia wanted me to go with her to look after her and now I'm leaving her open to an attack from this gigolo. But she's a grown woman and I'm not a babysitter, right? *Well, now I sound like a stroppy child.*

"Stay safe," I tell her again before walking out of the restaurant. I give the wanker a stern look but he ignores me; his complete focus is on Bri. *Oh, I fucking hate this.*

When I get back to my room I jump in the shower and let the warm water wash away the day. This is only day two of our journey and I'm already fretting over Bri. Khalid and his stupid talk have me completely muddled up and turned me into some protective alpha-hole and I need to cut it out because otherwise I'll drive her and me bonkers. Especially if I get between her and her mission. If I know anything about her it's that she will make it happen, come what may.

It's her decision, right? I was never concerned when Ben made me drive him and one of his many hook ups back to his house and there's no difference here really. But then I never—never mind. I need some sleep. That's what I need!

I must have drifted off as a loud bang wakes me up. It's coming from next door: Bri's room. She's giggling. I would recognise that giggle anywhere. The walls are thin as paper and I can hear mumbled words and laughter. How is it that I always end up lying and listening to other people fuck?

Well, they're not really fucking yet. They're just giggling. But if she brought him back to her room I know what to expect.

He has a phony laugh and if I didn't already think he's a twat, I would now.

I don't know what he's doing but I hear Bri say, "Saucy," followed by more laughter.

Earplugs, I need my earplugs. I dig through my bag but come up empty. I must have left them at home. *There's no way I can listen to this.* I swing my legs out of the bed and slip on my tracksuit bottoms and a T-shirt. I hear Bri moan as I tie my trainers. *Nope, enough is enough.* I don't need that. From tomorrow onwards I'm going to insist that our rooms are not next to each other. I grab the key from the table and leave. Time for a midnight run.

Eleven

Il pene della savana

The Bush Dick

Bridget

OKAY. THAT FEELS QUITE nice. Giovanni's lips are sliding over my neck. He keeps poking his tongue out though and I'm not quite sure about that. Feels quite... stabby... weird.

As predicted, once Omar left the restaurant Giovanni came over and joined me at the table. He made a big fuss about me being from England, how much he loves England, and how he loves London even more. I tried to explain to him that I'm not from London, but he wasn't listening.

He was funny though. We had a few drinks, we laughed. Well, I giggled and he was mainly telling me how beautiful I am. And how desirable. I know it was all bollocks but

I lapped it up all the same. It's just difficult to resist the charming Italian way.

He moved closer and closer to me until his chair was no longer opposite but next to me. And I didn't stop him when he kissed me. I didn't really want to stop him.

He tasted like wine and something else I couldn't identify. It was a good kiss. And my hormones were like, "Yay, let the sexy time begin!" And so I threw caution to the wind and after I paid, we went for a stroll. But there wasn't really much to see in this part of Milan. So, somehow, we ended up back at my room.

"Are you into kinky stuff?" Giovanni groans against my lips. It sounds much sexier with an Italian accent than if a guy back home said it. Can you imagine a Scouser saying "D'ya like kinky secks, love"? I have to hold back a giggle at the thought. But the Italian accent, well, it just gives women worldwide a metaphorical boner.

Giovanni gives me a wink that doesn't quite have the same impact that Omar's winks have—

Woah let's get him out of my head, right away. I wanted this, didn't I?

I shrug at Giovanni's question and apparently that means yes here in Italy. He takes my hand and puts it on his back pocket.

"Pull it out," he whispers in my ear. At first I thought he wanted me to grab his arse, but then I realised he has something hard and metal in his back pocket. Like some metal hoops. *What is this?*

Giovanni nibbles on my neck again before moaning, "If you like kinky stuff, you're gonna like this."

Oh jeez is he a pleasure dom as well, like Ben? My friend Amelia met her boyfriend on a BDSM dating app and he turned out to be a pleasure dom. Something I had to google when she told us about it because I'd never heard of it.

"Come on, *bellissima*," he groans in my ear. I'm a little bit concerned about what he has planned but also intrigued, so I reach into Giovanni's back pocket and pull out the metal loops. Handcuffs.

"You like?" he asks and wiggles his eyebrows.

"To be honest, I'm not quite sure how I feel about being handcuffed by a complete stranger," I mumble. *Who the fuck walks around with handcuffs?*

"No, no, no, darling. These are for me," he purrs. I stare at him.

"You want me to tie you up?"

"Yes. I like it. When I'm tied to a bed and the woman... what do you call it? Sucks me off?"

Apparently we are done whispering sweet nothings in my ear and instead we are onto hardcore dirty talk. *Is that what one-night-stands are like these days?* Maybe I should ask Omar.

I'm still not one hundred percent sure that handcuffs are a normal thing to bring to a hook up but each to their own. There are some niggly doubts in my tummy but my very excited pussy is telling them to bugger off because she wants to have some fun.

Giovanni nibbles my earlobe and my girly bits take notice and definitely want to get into the action. *Surely if I give him a blowie I'll get something in return?*

He guides me to the bed before starting to undress himself. I just stand there and gawk at him. I mean, he's shaped like a Greek god, Roman god—well, some deity. Defined muscles, sprinkled with dark hair, leading down to—oh, a moderately sized, hard cock sticking out from a bushy nest of hair. That's all I can call it. This god is one hairy beast down there. I have to bite my lip to not giggle because it does look funny. Like a giraffe lifting his head out of the bushes on the Savannah.

Giovanni takes my hesitation as shyness. He reaches for my hand and slides it over his dick. "Like this darling," he whispers in my ear.

Ohh thanks, you twerp. I'm only 44 years old. I think I do know how to touch a man. I want to tell him that but then he nibbles on my neck again. And I love that so much that I moan loudly.

Eventually he crawls onto the bed and lies down on his back. He lifts his arms above his head close to the headboard and whispers seductively, "Tie me up, darling."

Right. Let's get this over with. I feel a bit weird when, fully dressed, I restrain a naked god to the bedframe, but here we are. The handcuffs are simple ones without a lock, you just press a button to undo them. Friends of mine gave me similar ones as a as a joke for my birthday one year. I tried to get my ex to use them on me but he wasn't interested.

"Right, darling? Suck me off!" Giovanni demands after the handcuffs click shut.

Alright, let's do this. Maybe I should have asked him first what I'll get in return. But when in Rome... or when in Milan—

I start to kiss my way slowly downwards but he just urges me on to go straight for the target. As I slide my lips over his cock, he groans. I mean, I guess the good thing with him being tied up is he can't push me down, right? Although I'm not sure there would be much of a risk of gagging on the bush-dick.

Apparently a fully dressed English woman licking his cock really does it for the Italian god because it doesn't take very long for him to cry out and spew—without warning I would like to point out—his funky tasting spunk into my mouth. It tastes odd and for a second I keep it there, curious to find out what the taste reminds me off, until I realise what the fuck I'm doing and swallow hard to get rid of it.

"That was wonderful, darling," he sighs. I don't think I can say the same with that taste still lingering in my mouth. I wonder if there is a way I can get some water without him feeling offended.

I unclick his handcuffs and drop onto the bed next to him hoping to get something in return. "Thank you, darling." Giovanni gives me a quick peck on the lips before sliding off the bed and pulling his trousers back on.

"Are you leaving?"

"It's late."

"What about me?" I blurt out. My pussy is joining into the protest.

"Ohh. Umm. I'm tired now."

"So you mean you got what you wanted and you don't need to return anything?"

"Ah, darling, next time," he says before waving one last time and sneaking out of my room.

Well, thanks for nothing you twat. We both know there isn't going to be a next time. He and his bush-dick can go and fuck themselves as far as I'm concerned.

For a second I wonder if I should just take things into my own hand, so to speak. But I'm not really in the mood anymore. I stare at the handcuffs that he left behind in his hasty retreat.

So much for having some fun in Italy. I just hope the next bush-dick will find his way inside me.

Twelve

L'a fuga romantica

The Holiday Romance

Omar

BRI IS STUFFING A croissant into her mouth as I approach the table in the breakfast room. "Morning," I try to be cheerful despite what happened yesterday.

When I got back from my run last night it was quiet next door, so I assume knobhead didn't have a lot of stamina; I wasn't gone that long. Did that fill me with glee? Maybe.

"Morning," Bri mumbles through a mouthful of pastry.

"Good evening?" I ask because I'm an arsehole. She just rolls her eyes in response but doesn't say anything else. I'm not sure why I'm torturing myself. *Why am I pushing her on it?*

"When did it become normal for guys to ask for a blowjob on a one-night-stand and then bugger off?" She stares at me like I represent the evil in all men.

"What do you mean?"

"I'm talking about the plonker with a small knob, who took what he needed and then left me high and dry."

Okay, wow. She says it as it is without holding back, I have to give her that.

"I'm sorry, I guess," I offer an apology that isn't mine to give. "I did think he was wanker," I add and hide my smirk behind the cup of coffee I'm lifting to my lips. There's the alpha-hole in me again, raising his fist with joy that that knobhead didn't touch her.

"What made you think that? You didn't even speak to him?" Bri takes another large bite from her chocolate croissant.

"A guy that hits on a woman who's with another man is a wanker. He didn't know our relationship but he flirted with you over my shoulder anyway."

"You could have said something yesterday." Apparently we're not done taking out her frustrations on me.

"Would you have believed me?" I retort. "No. And it wasn't my place."

"Hmm," is the only answer I get.

"Anyhow. What're we doing today?"

By the time we get back from sightseeing Bri looks absolutely knackered. We didn't bother with the car since everything's within walking distance but that meant we were on our feet all day. And let's not forget the climb to the rooftop of the Duomo—two hundred and fifty stairs! Of course once we reached the top we realised there's a lift we could've taken. Bri had a few choice words for me, but as soon as she saw the view all was forgiven.

However, now even her enthusiasm can't disguise her lack of energy. *I guess picking up Italian stallions is not on the table tonight.*

"I know where we're going now," I announce.

"Please let it be our hotel. I need to shower and lie down for a bit," Bri groans.

"Better! Come on." I grab her hand and pull her across the busy road. It's only when we get to the other side that I realise what I'm doing and let her fingers slide from my grasp. She doesn't say anything, but I can see her eyeing me.

Keep it together. We're not friends, we're not lovers. I'm her driver. She's my boss.

We walk through the main archway into Milano Centrale station. Bri gasps at the imposing entrance hall but I guide her to the left through an inconspicuous dark wood door. You wouldn't expect much, and certainly not the long hall full of food stalls. A wall of noise greets us and the scent of all the food is almost overpowering.

Bri's eyes widen as she takes in the sea of pastries and macaroons. There are vitrines filled with sandwiches and shelves lined with glasses of tiramisu and an Italian variation of strawberries and cream. People are crowding the small tables, drinking espresso and enjoying each other's company.

"Oh my God, that looks so delicious!" Bri exclaims. She seems to have forgotten her tiredness as she moves from one stall to the next. In the end we decide to get a tiramisu and a strawberry and cream and to eat half and half again. There are no tables available so we take our desserts back out into the stations entrance hall and take a seat between two imposing stone pillars. "I think I've died and gone to heaven," Bri moans as she licks tiramisu off her spoon before dipping it in the glass I'm holding and scooping out a healthy portion of sponge, cream and strawberries. She lifts it to her pale red lips and drags it off her spoon with gusto. I'm mesmerised and nearly groan when the tip of her tongue pokes out and licks some of the cream from the corner of her mouth.

Wow, I'm in so much trouble. I avert my eyes and clear my throat.

"Was it worth coming here?" I ask before devouring a spoonful of tiramisu myself.

"So worth it," she grins between bites. "Thank you, Omar!"

"You're welcome!" If she's happy, I'm happy.

"Oh my God. Look over there." Bri points at a building to our left.

We arrived in Florence two days ago after a brief twenty-four hours in Pisa. In general we're encountering less tourists than we would have in the summer but Pisa was an exception. We were wondering if there was something going on in the city as there were so many people but the receptionist assured us *Affari come al solito*—business as usual.

It was just too much and Bri decided we should move on to Florence, and since we arrived she's been back to her joyful self. I can't blame her. Florence is one of my favourite places in Italy, only surpassed by Rome.

Yesterday I took her to see Michelangelo's David which was on her bucket list. I contacted a friend of mine who has a friend who has a brother—that's how things work here—who works as the head of security at the museum. He managed to get us in ahead of the crowds. Bri just sat there for half an hour, in her own world and not saying a word, just studying the statue.

On the other hand I couldn't take my eyes of her. Seeing the emotions she was going through in her expressions. It was captivating. Her ex should be hung up by his balls for not giving this woman what she always wanted.

When the museum opened its doors to the crowd we left and spent the day hanging around in coffee shops, soaking up the atmosphere. Bri's not your typical tourist with a tick list of all the highlights in a city that she must see which I love about her. She prefers to just sit there and watch people and listen to conversations, even if she doesn't understand them. Every so often she'll ask me in a hushed tone to translate what people are saying. Usually when she thinks they are arguing or flirting. When I lean in to whisper the translation in her ear I pick up the gentle scent of lemons. It's too subtle to be perfume, so I'm guessing it's her shower gel or shampoo. But it's so her that I know, from now on, the smell of lemons will always conjure up memories of our time together.

I also don't seem to be able to help myself from turning into a possessive wanker whenever one of those "Italian stallions" casts his eyes over her. Luckily, she's oblivious to the admiration she draws, but I'm not and whenever I notice it I gently put my hand on her lower back or lean in to whisper something in her ear. Bri gives me odd looks when I do but I've convinced myself that I'm keeping the wankers away from her because Ben and Amelia asked me to look after her. That's my story and I'm sticking to it.

Today is our last day in Florence and Bri wanted to do one of the bus tours. I know the city well so I don't expect to see a lot of new things but when she looked at me with sparkling eyes and big grin I couldn't say no to a sightseeing tour.

The bus slowly makes its way up the steep road on the slopes of Monte alle Croci. I know exactly where we're heading and Bri is going to love it.

"Oh, oh, look, look." She points between the trees where you can see little glimpses of the city beneath us. I say nothing because I don't want to spoil the surprise for her. The bus snakes its way up the hill whilst Bri desperately tries to take a snap of the city through the tree line.

One bend... another bend... ahead I can already see the trees clearing and I can't hold back a grin.

Finally, we break through the trees and the bus rolls along Piazzale Michelangelo. It's a large elevated terrace and the most spectacular viewpoint of Florence. In the centre of the Piazzale is a replica statue of David and at the western end are steps leading to a restaurant.

Bri gasps as she takes it all in and then turns to me with wide eyes.

"Can we get off, please? Can we get off?" she asks. I nod as the bus pulls into the stop. We unplug our headphones and head to the lower deck.

"Thank you," Bri shouts to the bus driver before hopping off. A cool wind hits us in the face but the sun is shining to counteract the cold a little.

We walk the short distance to the stairs at the western end where there's the most spectacular view. Bri leans against the banister surrounding the square and soaks up the view of the whole city spread in front of us. The Cathedral of Santa Maria del Fiore looms above the surrounding houses, its grandeur impossible to miss. Off to the left, the River Arno winds its way through the city. The iconic Ponte Vecchio, a bridge lined with shops and houses that seem to cling to it, spans the river.

"Why did you not tell me?" Bri gently smacks my upper arm. "This is amazing."

"I know. It's beautiful, isn't it? I wanted you to be surprised," I grin.

Bri takes a seat on the steps and I join her. The wind is less fierce here and the sun has a chance to warm us up.

"I think this is one of my highlights so far," she declares.

"I never get tired of this view. Florence is one of my favourite cities."

"I think it's one of mine now too." She gives me another big smile before we both fall silent and just enjoy the view.

When I look over at her she seems lost in thoughts and there's something dark in her expression.

"What are you thinking?"

"I... I was just thinking about Giovanni."

"The guy from Milan?" The alpha-hole in me roars. *Okay, no need for jealousy.*

"Yeah," she shrugs. "You know, I think that at forty-four I'm entitled to have some fun and you hear so many stories about Italian men. But the fact that he just took what he needed and then left... it kind of puts me off trying again."

"Not everyone is a weasel like that knobhead," I reply but the alpha-hole in me is jubilant.

"You know, I'm not looking for a relationship. In fact, I don't want a relationship. But someone who isn't just in for their own gain would be nice. Unlike bush-dick—"

"Excuse me?"

"He had a moderate dick surrounded by a lot of bush," she giggles and I can't hold back the laughter. This woman is crazy, in a good way.

"Sounds to me like you're after more than just a one-night-stand. You're looking for a holiday romance. Someone who wants to spend time with you, who cares for you and doesn't just see you as a mouth to... you know—"

"Fuck."

"Yes, that. A romance where you both agree it's just for the holidays."

"Maybe. Tough to do when you travel from one city to the next every two days."

Offer yourself, offer yourself, idiot! I try to ignore my dick and remind myself yet again that this isn't going to happen.

There's a brief moment of silence before she turns to me.

“Or are you talking about yourself?” I don’t know which of us appears more shocked.

“Me? No, no, no. Sorry. No, I didn't mean me. I didn't... I definitely didn't,” I stutter.

“Okay, no need to fight me quite that hard,” she laughs, embarrassed.

“No, you misunderstand. You’re a beautiful woman. Any guy would be lucky to be with you. But I'm your employee.”

“Well, technically you’re Ben’s employee.”

Neither of us says anything further. For a second I’m actually considering it. But shagging her is far from what I promised Ben and Amelia.

“What should I get us? Ice cream?” I try to lighten the mood. Bri looks like she wants to say more on the topic of dating but lets it go and just nods in agreement.

All I can think about as I walk to the little snack van is that that was my chance for... *no, it’s definitely not the right thing to do*. But doing the wrong thing has never felt so enticing.

Thirteen

L'esorcista

The Exorcist

Bridget

My little beautiful Bella is just lying there licking her arsehole whilst I try to catch her up on everything we've seen today. I'm not sure if she's even aware that I'm here but I love looking at her and telling her about my day. I would just prefer a better view than her bumhole.

Obviously I censor what I tell her because I'm pretty sure Amelia and Ben are listening in the background so I can't really spill the beans on bush-dick or that Omar is... *roar*, for a lack of a better word.

So far I've managed to talk to her every day. Omar keeps grumbling about it, yet he's always at the lookout for Wi-Fi when we get close to four in the afternoon. Today is our last day in Florence so we headed back to the hotel for me to call Bella before packing. My room is a bit of a tip really, but I unpacked everything I brought with me, planning to put together one bag for the next few days so poor Omar doesn't have to schlepp all my suitcases to my room.

"And then, Bella, we went up onto this hill and it had this amazing view, and I could see the Ponte Vecchio and the cathedral and—" A wave of nausea hits me and I hold still for a moment in the hope it will pass. I take a deep breath and my stomach settles. *I wonder what that was.* I'm really not feeling very well. I try to lie very still and—

Oh my God. I scramble off the bed as quickly as I can. I already taste the first of the vomit in my mouth. I rush to the bathroom and bend over the toilet and—

Omar

I don't know what it is with this country and paper-thin hotel walls, but it's like every room's made of cardboard. I'm stepping out of the shower when I hear it—the awful, gut-wrenching sounds coming from next door. It's Bri's room, and the relentless retching noise leaves no doubt about what's happening.

I quickly throw on some shorts and a T-shirt, my heart thudding in my chest. She's still throwing up, and I'm really starting to worry. I rush to her door, but as I raise my hand to knock, I hesitate. What if I'm invading her privacy just when she needs space?

But the awful sound of her heaving doesn't stop and I can't just stand here doing nothing. I knock once and there's no reply. I knock again, more urgently this time, but there's still no response—just the sound of her struggling. I'm torn between the need to respect her privacy and fear that she might really need help. "Bri?" I call out. No answer. I press the door handle and it opens. Luckily this is one of those hotels with old fashioned keys rather than modern keycards and she has forgotten to lock the door after herself again despite me reminding her every day.

"Bri," I call one more time and am answered by gagging. Her tablet is on the bed with a live video call of her cat who seems to be grooming herself, completely oblivious to what's going on.

I ignore the tablet and step into the bathroom.

"Bri are you okay?"

"Go, go away. Don't. Don't look at me," she manages to moan before another wave of sickness hits her. "I'm dying," she mumbles between gagging and throwing up. "Omar, talk to—" She gags but nothing comes out, "talk to Bella."

"Your cat?"

"Yes, please."

"Why?"

"She'll be worried."

"It's a cat."

"Plea—" More gagging. I decide now isn't the time to argue with her so I head back to the bedroom and pick up the tablet.

"Hey, cat." The tabby furball looks at the screen. *Huh, maybe she does pay attention*

"Well listen, Bri is ill so we'll have to cut this short. But I'll take good care of her." *Fucking hell, I'm talking to a cat.*

"Oh my god is she okay?" a voice shouts before the table on the other end of the call is moved. Amelia appears on the screen.

"Yes, no, I don't know yet. It only just started. Probably food poisoning. I should go and look after her." I point to the bathroom. Not that Amelia can see what I'm pointing at.

"Of course. Please keep us posted." She gives me a worried smile before the call is ended.

Bri snaps at me again the minute I step into the bathroom, "Please don't look at me. Just leave me to it. I'll be fine."

"Bri, let me be here for you." She looks white as a sheet and her forehead is covered in sweat as she grabs the toilet seat again. I pick up a small towel from the sink and run it under the cold tap. Sitting next to her on the floor, I gently wipe her forehead to cool her down.

"You really shouldn't be seeing this," she mumbles. She looks already exhausted.

"I'm here for you, okay? Do you think it's food poisoning or a virus?"

"I don't—" More retching but she has nothing left in her stomach to bring up. "I don't know."

"You did have those oysters that didn't look that nice."

She doesn't reply but instead starts to dry heave. I gently rub her back and wipe her face with the cold towel. It's another half an hour before her stomach seems to have settled a bit. She's hunched over the toilet and I carefully lift her in my arms and carry her to the bed.

She curls up under the duvet. I can't resist stroking her hair away from her sweaty forehead. She looks drained and done for.

I try to give her some water but she's too weak.

"Come on, Bri. Just a sip." I lift her head gently, holding a bottle of cold water to her lips. She slowly takes a few drops and when she's done I carefully place her head back onto the pillow. Her forehead is damp with sweat, and her normally bright eyes are dull and tired. Worry gnaws at me so I press the button on the phone and call reception. My voice is tense as I quickly explain what's happening, and the receptionist offers to call for medical help.

"Bri, the doctor's on the way."

"Ohh, I don't need a doctor," she murmurs weakly.

"Yes, yes, you do. This isn't okay. We need to make sure it's not something serious."

She's lying on the bed looking fragile, her body small and vulnerable under the covers. I sit beside her, holding her hand and feeling helpless as I wait. The minutes drag by, each one stretching endlessly. Finally, after what feels like forever but is only forty-five minutes, the receptionist calls up to say the doctor's here. He is an older man, with the urgency of a snail when he enters the room. He takes one long look at Bri, asks me a few questions and then casually explains it's probably food poisoning. He advises me to keep her hydrated and if she doesn't improve within twenty-four hours, to take her to the local hospital. He is telling me what I already suspected. I'm not sure it was worth calling him out, but at least I feel like I'm doing everything I can.

Another wave of nausea hits Bri just after the doctor leaves and she rushes to the bathroom. I follow her, rubbing her back as she retches. Her stomach is empty so she's just throwing up the water I gave her earlier. Her body shakes with effort, and it breaks my heart to see her like this. Once it passes I guide her back to bed and offer her a bit more water. She might throw it up again, but her body needs fluids. The doctor also left some electrolytes so I add them to the bottle. She takes a few sips, her hand trembling, before collapsing back onto the bed.

I lie down next to her, feeling the warmth of her body next to mine. She curls up next to me, resting her head on my chest. It feels right, like she's where she's meant to be. I shouldn't say it, I shouldn't even think it, but it feels so natural. I stroke her hair gently, my fingers tracing soothing patterns.

"Just rest now," I whisper. "You're going to be alright."

Her breathing slows and deepens as she finally falls asleep, her face peaceful. I listen to her steady breaths, feeling a sense of relief wash over me. Maybe she's over the worst of it. Holding her close, I shut my eyes and let myself relax for the first time since this all started.

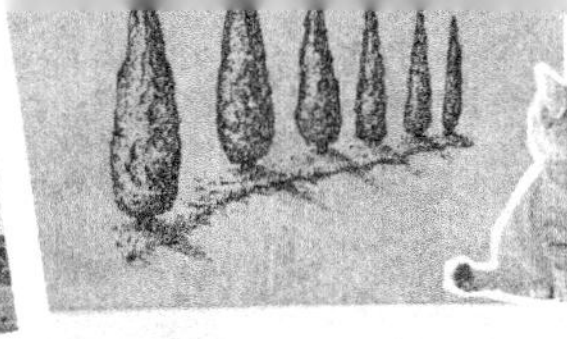

Fourteen

Il marito

The Husband

Omar

I DON'T LIKE THIS at all. There's a red symbol blinking on the dashboard. And now there's another one blinking. So much for bloody German cars. The engine stutters and I let the car roll to a standstill at the side of the road. Luckily we're not on a motorway; we've just been cruising along the coastal road towards Grosseto. We were planning to stop off in some of the little villages along the way but the car started to make funny noises.

We're on the outskirts of Castiglioncello and I can see the roofs of the first houses in the distance.

"Wait, why are we stopping?" Bri asks with concern. There's colour back in her cheeks, and her eyes are lively again. We had to stay an extra two days in Florence until she felt well enough to travel but she's truly on the mend, judging by the gusto with which she's been demolishing her travel snacks.

The unplanned extension has put us a little behind our schedule, especially as Bri wants to travel via Salzburg on the way back home. Seeing the Christmas market there is top of her list.

We decided to only stop once on the way to Rome, in Grosseto. This should have compensated for the time we lost in Florence but the car playing up might mean we're behind schedule again.

"The car's died," I reply, frustration creeping into my voice. I turn the key but nothing happens. I try again—still nothing. "I think we've got a problem," I state the bloody obvious. Bri looks at me expectantly, as if I can just fix it.

"So what are you gonna do?" she asks.

"Me?"

"You're the driver."

"Yes, but I'm not a mechanic. There's only so much I can do," I shrug. Bri leans back in the passenger seat and sighs.

"We'll have to park it here, walk into the village, and find someone to help us," I suggest.

"I can wait with the car," Bri says.

"Or you can come with me. It's only a short walk, and I'd feel better if you weren't left on your own by the side of the road."

"It's broad daylight. What's going happen to me?"

"You never know."

"Nothing's going to happen."

"Come on, Bri. It's only a short walk." I give her a pleading look. I really don't want her to stay out here on her own. Alpha-hole alert.

"Fine." She grabs her little handbag, the one that's so small I wonder why she even has it. You can barely fit a phone in it. We start walking down the road to the village. Today is Sunday, so finding a mechanic who's open is probably going to be impossible, but we can give it a try. And if not, we might be able to at least get a bed and breakfast, stay the night, and get the car fixed tomorrow.

The sun casts a warm glow over everything, making the terracotta rooftops of Castiglioncello look like a postcard. The sea glistens in the distance, and the gentle sound of waves crashing adds a soothing backdrop to our steps.

After a short walk we find a cosy café with tables set outside under large umbrellas. We approach the waiter, a friendly young man with a warm smile.

"Mi scusi, conosce un'officina meccanica qui vicino?" I ask him for the nearest car repair shop.

He frowns slightly before explaining that there isn't one in Castiglioncello. There is one in the next village, though.

"That's not going to do us any bloody good," I mutter under my breath.

"What did he say?" Bri asks, looking at me with a mix of curiosity and concern.

"Nearest repair shop is in the next village. It's Sunday in Italy. They're probably closed, so why don't we look for a bed and breakfast? Maybe someone there can give me a lift to tow the car back to the B&B. Then we can call the mechanic tomorrow to see if he can come over, or if we can get someone to take us to him. If a certain person had signed up with the AA, then of course, it would be easier."

"Oh my God don't start again," she protests. I gave her a hard time when she showed me the Beast for the first time because she hadn't signed up for breakdown cover.

The waiter kindly points us up the hill. "*Il B&B più vicino è proprio lì in cima,*" he says, gesturing with a smile.

I glance up the steep incline and then back at the waiter. He assures me it's not a long walk and wishes us a good stay in Castiglioncello.

"So?" Bri tries to get me to translate our conversation.

"There's a B&B up on the hill. It's not too far, apparently."

Bri looks at me and sighs. "Alright, let's give it a go."

As we start the climb, Bri mutters, "I hope it's worth it."

♥

"Oh my God, this is so steep," Bri breathes heavily behind me as we climb. When I turn around I see her hair sticking to her forehead with sweat, her face bright red, and she's blowing hard.

"We're almost there, Snaily," I tease.

She shoots me a playful glare, then walks past me, her determination shining through her exhaustion.

When we finally reach the top we find a charming B&B nestled amongst olive trees. Its rustic stone walls and cosy balconies look inviting.

We're greeted by an elderly woman with kind eyes and a welcoming smile.

"*Buongiorno.*"

"*Buongiorno. La nostra macchina si è rotta e dobbiamo portarla da un meccanico domani. Avete delle stanze disponibili e magari qualcuno che possa aiutarmi a trainare la macchina fin qui?*" I explain our situation to her.

"*Certamente, ho una camera per te e tua moglie,*" she replies with a kind smile. *One room only, for me and my wife. Fuck! What now?*

I can see a statue of the Virgin Mary on one of the window seats. *Desperate times, desperate measures.*

"*Perfetto*", I tell her and she waves for us to follow her.

"Oh, she has rooms?" Bri asks.

"One room."

"One... one room?" Bri stares at me. I just shrug. *She's not going to like this.*

"Didn't you explain that we can't share a room?" she asks.

"She... she thinks we're married," I whisper as we climb the stairs to the upper floor of the building.

"Excuse me!" Bri exclaims.

"I know these Italian grannies. They won't let us stay in one room unless we're married."

"Well... I don't want to stay in a room with you," she blows out making her fringe fly.

"What other choice do we have?" I ask. Before Bri can reply the old lady pulls us from our thoughts.

"*Eccomi qui. Questa è la vostra camera. Mi chiamo Cecilia. Se c'è qualche cosa che posso fare per aiutarvi, fatemelo sapere. E Francesco, uno dei miei fidanzati, può aiutarvi con la macchina.*"

"*Uno dei tuoi fidanzati?*"

"*Sì*," she giggles.

"Argh, what's she saying?" Bri begs me to translate.

"One of her boyfriends will help me with the car."

"One of... she has more than one boyfriend."

"Apparently," I shrug. *I'm such an idiot. How could I fall for a stupid stereotype?*

"Unbelievable," Bri sighs. "Are you *now* going to tell her the truth?"

"How can I? How embarrassing would that be?" I hiss under my breath. "It's only one night. Besides, it doesn't change that she's only got one room available."

Cecilia is studying us. God, I hope she doesn't speak English because she'll think I'm a complete numpty.

"*Cecilia, sono Omar e questa è Bri*," I introduce us. Bri waves awkwardly before giving Cecilia a big smile and stepping into the cosy room.

"Husband, why don't you get me my luggage?" Bri smirks at me and falls onto the mattress.

"Yes, honey bunny," I reply and follow the old lady before Bri can say anything else. *OK, this time I've got us into a right mess.*

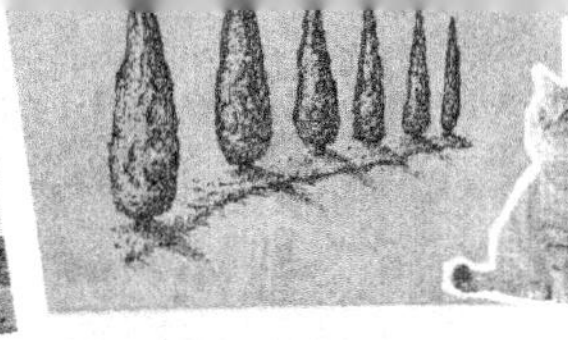

Fifteen

Gli eremiti dell'amore

The Love Hermits

Bridget

I'VE DIED AND GONE to heaven. It might be because it's the first decent food I've had in days—Omar made me stick to bread and other dry stuff once I stopped resembling Regan from The Exorcist.

I take another large bite of the Pizza Margarita and the cheesy goodness melts in my mouth.

"Fuck, that's good," Omar moans opposite me. After Maurizio, one of Cecilia's boyfriends, helped Omar to get the car back to the B&B we went in search of food. There are plenty of restaurants overlooking the bay, but as we have done for most of our trip, we avoided the obvious tourist traps and found a tiny place two streets over from our accommodation instead.

There're no linen napkins or menus in five different languages, but therefore it has the authentic feel of a little family run ristorante, and hands down the best pizza in the world.

"So good," I agree with Omar. I fold another slice in half and lift it to my mouth. Omar thought he'd be teaching me something new when we had our first pizza in Milan and I had to explain that I love old movies from the 50s and 60s, and I learned the pizza folding trick from the glorious Sophia Loren. I adore her and Cary Grant in *Houseboat*. I recapped almost the whole film and it was one of many times when Omar just looked at me with an unreadable expression. I swear he thinks I'm a weirdo.

We finish our pizza in silence only broken by the occasional moan. I didn't think I was that hungry but once the Margherita pizza was in front of me I practically inhaled the whole thing.

"*Ti è piaciuto il pasto?*" the young waitress asks as she clears the table.

"*Sì, grazie*," Omar replies. "She wanted to know if you enjoyed your meal," he explains for my benefit. I give the waitress a big smile and nod enthusiastically.

She leaves and we fall silent. Omar fiddles with the glass in his hand, avoiding my eyes. I want to know what's going on his head but I'm not sure if I can ask.

"Bri..." he breaks the silence, "I really want to apologise for causing such a mess. It was a ridiculous idea and I've no clue why I thought it was smart to say we're married." He gives me a sheepish look. "You know when you open your mouth before you think? It was that kind of situation. I just thought we need a room and—"

"And you fell foul of a stupid stereotype." I finish for him. "I'm surprised given how much you have travelled, I thought you'd be more openminded." I lean back and take a sip from my wine.

"We all have our prejudices, as much as we don't want to," he replies.

"Wise beyond your age," I giggle.

"You make it sound like I'm in my twenties. I'm a very mature thirty-nine-year-old student," he objects with a grin. "We're practically the same age."

"Well, not quite. When you were born I was the advanced aged of five, learning to write." I reply with a shrug.

"That's an odd way of looking at it. Besides, you may be ahead of me in age but I make up for it with the life experience I've gathered on my travels." His eyes are locked on me, with amusement but also something else, something like determination to prove me wrong.

"*Qualcosa di dolce?*" the waitress interrupts and holds out a small menu.

Omar leans forward and says with an edge in his voice, "She asked if you want something sweet." There is something so intense in his eyes, I have to swallow hard as all sorts of images come to my mind... naughty thoughts.

I accept the menu but don't look at it. I stay focused on Omar.

"*Due tiramisù, per favore,*" he says to the waitress without taking his eyes of me.

"Who says I want tiramisu?" I ask him after the waitress heads back to the kitchen.

"We have been in this country for two weeks and you've always had tiramisu," he beams at me triumphantly. He's right, of course he's right. But I desperately want to wipe that smug look off his face. It unsettles me when he takes control. Not in a bad way, in a way that makes me squeeze my thighs together to stop that pulsing in my core.

"I guess a husband knows best," I say before draining the last of the wine from my glass. That does the trick.

"I deserved that," he mumbles and ruffles his hair. When he's done it sticks up wildly and I want to slide my fingers through to put it back in place.

"It's okay, I'm sure we'll survive one night," I shrug. "Can I ask you something Omar?"

"Sure." His hands are calmly folded on the table in front of him. I've noticed that not much rattles him. Well, aside from when I turn into a vomit spewing entity or when he has to lie.

"Why are you such a defender of singledom? Most people our age at least have a tragic or less tragic divorce story to tell. But you seem to be determined to not go anywhere near relationships." He doesn't talk a lot about himself but he has made that point abundantly clear.

"I—" He's interrupted as the waitress places enormous portions of tiramisu in front of us. I shuffle a spoonful into my mouth before she's even had the chance to walk away.

"Oh, wow. I'm having a food orgasm," I moan. Omar's expression changes, he looks more tense and I swear his pupils expand. "Sorry, you were saying?" I prompt him.

"I've seen first-hand that happily ever afters don't exist and I just have no interest in dealing with heartbreak." I study him as he shifts his focus to his dessert and devours a spoonful of deliciousness.

"Someone broke you heart?" I ask.

"My dad didn't just leave us, he decided one woman wasn't enough for him and cheated on my mum when I was sixteen. She offered to give him a chance if he gave up the other woman. I guess she was still in love with him, despite everything. He left a week later saying he wasn't a one woman man." He drops his spoon to the plate and takes a sip of water.

"I'm sorry. And because of that you think happy relationships don't exist?" I probe tentatively.

"I'm a cheater as well. I'm like him."

I wait for him to say more but he takes a spoonful of tiramisu.

"Yeah, I need more here." He can't just drop a bomb like that on me and leave it.

"I... it's stupid. I was eighteen or nineteen, I had a girlfriend. We weren't really serious, when you're eighteen how serious can it really be? But nevertheless we were in a relationship and I cheated on her. I went to a party without her and fooled around with another woman."

"And?"

"I broke up with Sonja and promised myself no relationships. I'm as toxic as my dad."

"A tad dramatic, don't you think? For a start you learned from your mistake and he clearly didn't." I scoop the last spoonful of tiramisu up with a tiny bit of sadness. Despite being full I wish it would never end.

"Maybe. I don't know. But look around and everyone is getting divorced or breaking up. No relationship lasts forever."

"Well, I know plenty of happy couples, Amelia and Ben, Lizzie and Coop, your cousins all seem to be very happy," I object.

"Yes, and my mum and her boyfriend, and Russ and his girlfriend. For now. Who knows how long it'll last" he objects. There is genuine conviction in his face.

"Let me ask you something. You like going on holiday, right?"

"Yes," he replies, puzzled.

"Well you know holidays will end eventually you can still enjoy them, learn from them, take pleasure from them. Even if a relationship doesn't last forever, don't you think you can enjoy it while it lasts? Can it not enrich your life?" *Why do I feel like a hypocrite?*

Omar's eyes find mine, "I... I guess, maybe... hang on, didn't you also say that you don't want a relationship?" *Oh, yes, that's why I'm a bloody hypocrite.*

"We're not talking about me," I object weakly.

"Tell me how your situation is different from mine?" he challenges with a smirk.

"I... my marriage was good and I got two amazing children out of it," I defend myself.

"And yet you say you no longer want a relationship." He won't let me off the hook that easily.

"A woman can decide that she wants to be single," I try the feminist route.

"Sure, but that's not what this is. You're also cynical about relationships," he points at me with a victorious grin.

Didn't I have similar concerns about Christopher and Ruthie's relationships?

"I think it's more that I'm concerned about getting hurt... about my kids getting hurt if it doesn't work out," I say quietly. I think this is the first time I've admitted this to myself.

"So you don't go on holiday either because you worry about it ending." Omar gives my hand a gentle squeeze.

"I guess we're both love hermits," I eventually say with a weak smile.

"Guess so," he returns my smile. I take a sip of wine contemplating what to say next. Having said what's holding me back from a new relationship out loud actually makes me quite sad. Maybe I don't want to be a hermit. We finish our wine in silence, lost in thought.

Omar is still frowning and for some reason I feel the urge to make him smile or cheer him up. I don't like seeing him so... sad.

"Look at us, we're in the land of *dolce vita* and *l'amore* and we are leading the anti-love coalition," I giggle but something has shifted between us. So many emotions and questions seem to swirl around. "For what it's worth, I'm glad I'm your first wife," I say and I'm not sure why.

Omar swallows hard before whispering, "Me too."

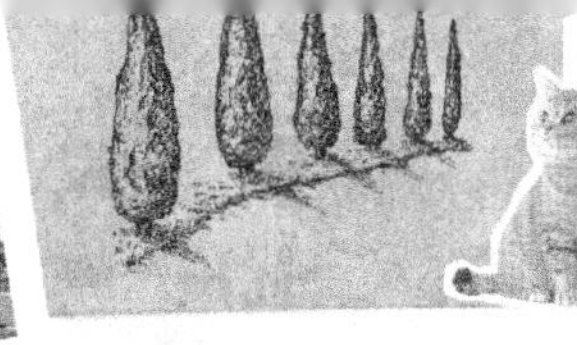

Sixteen

L'a prima volta

The First Time

Bridget

THE HOT WATER FEELS good on my skin and I stay under the spray for much longer than I need to. I eventually turn off the water, painfully aware that the only thing separating me in my nakedness from Omar is the tiny wooden door leading to the bedroom.

If we're lucky we can get *divorced* sooner rather than later, assuming the mechanic can fix the car tomorrow. Let's just hope it's not too bad and the trip isn't cut short. The thought causes me anxiety.

No, I'm not ready for this to be over. I won't let it be the end of the trip. If the car's broken I'll rent one. Yes, I'll just have a little less money left from Ruth, but that's okay. There, fixed it.

I pull on leggings and a tank top. Really, I should be wearing a bra as well but I can't sleep in one. Omar's eventually going to see the outline of my droopy boobies eventually, might as well scare him off right now. *I wonder if he dates women his age or younger, twenty something girlies with perky tits. How does he feel about older women?* And there's my mind in the gutter again. *Enough!*

I unlock the bathroom door and slip back into the bedroom. Omar is already in bed and the only light in the room comes from the small lamp on my nightstand. I can't help but steal glances at Omar's muscular frame outlined by his T-shirt. The way he's casually lounging on the bed sends shivers down my spine.

Omar rolls to his side, facing away from me. And I don't know if he's doing that to be polite or to make a point.

"Are you asleep?" I whisper.

"No, not yet."

"Do you think they're going to be able to fix the car tomorrow?"

"I don't know. I had a look and I can't see what the issue is and that makes it difficult to say how serious it is." His voice is muffled.

"Oh okay." I slide under the sheets and pull them up to my shoulders. *Why didn't we ask for a second blanket?*

We're on separate sides of the bed, facing away from each other.

"Night," I whisper into the room.

"Night," he replies. I reach to switch the lamp off but can't find the button. I tap the lamp thinking maybe it's one of the weird ones where you touch it's base and it turns off. Nothing. I find the end of the cable nearest to the lamp base and let my fingers slide along it to find the switch. Nothing.

"How do you switch this fucking thing off? I ask frustrated.

"The switch is at the lightbulb," Omar replies.

"Where? I can't find it."

"Bri!" He turns and leans over me. I lie flat on the mattress to give him space. I'm caged under him as he reaches out for the lamp, fiddles with it and switches it off.

The only light in the room is from the moon shining through the window. Omar hovers over me, his dark eyes are fixed on mine. I can feel the warmth of his body seep into me.

He lifts his hand and gently strokes a strand of hair from my face. His fingers brush my skin, soft but electric, sending a shiver through me. His eyes meet mine, and it feels like he's asking a question without saying a word. The space between us feels smaller and smaller, and somehow, it's like the world has slowed down, dragging out this moment and making my heart race.

He leans in lower, his breath warm against my cheek, and his body aligned perfectly with mine. I'm barely thinking straight as my fingers grab hold of his T-Shirt. I want this so much. I don't think I've ever wanted to kiss a man more than Omar.

But just as his lips are close enough to kiss, he mumbles, "Sorry," and rolls off me before turning and facing away from me again. *Noooo, come back!* My whole body screams. If I were braver, I'd take what I need from him but I'm not. I try to calm my breathing. Maybe it's for the best. No, not maybe! It's definitely for the better despite the formal complaint my vajayjay is planning to file with the European Court of Human Rights.

But no matter how hard I try to behave, as the silence falls over us my mind begins to wander to forbidden thoughts. *What would it be like to feel his lips on mine? To run my fingers through his thick black hair?* My heart speeds up again at the idea of crossing that line with him.

I draw in a sharp, steadying breath and scold myself for letting those fantasies invade my thoughts. This is dangerous territory; I will not jeopardize this trip just because I'm horny as hell. But no matter how hard I try to suppress these thoughts they continue to bubble beneath the surface.

I hear Omar's steady breathing next to me as he starts to fall asleep. This might be my only chance to indulge in these feelings without consequence; he'll never know what's going through my mind.

With cautious movements under the covers, I inch my hand lower until I can reach between my thighs. Heat radiates from within me as I press against the fabric of my leggings. Closing my eyes, I imagine its Omar's touch igniting this fire.

I let out a quiet gasp at the surge of pleasure that courses through me. The sound startles me, and I freeze, heart pounding in my chest. But when I steal a glance at Omar over my shoulder he's the same peaceful shadow as before. Relief washes over me, giving me the courage to continue with a bit of self-love.

I slip my hand beneath my waistband with bolder movements, finally feeling the silky wetness that's been building. A moan escapes my lips as I circle my fingertips around my sensitive clit. I press my face into the pillow to stifle any noises giving me away.

The room feels hot and heavy as the pleasure intensifies with each stroke. I can't believe I'm actually doing this beside him, but the thought only heightens the excitement coursing through me. The line between fantasy and reality blurs as my imagination runs wild.

Lost in my delicious thoughts, I don't notice that Omar's breathing has changed until it's too late.

Suddenly there's movement behind me as he turns towards me.

My hand freezes mid-motion as panic surges through me. Time stands still as I wait for words or actions—will he be angry? Disgusted? Or maybe he'll pretend like it never happened.

To my surprise, I feel his fingers gently stroking over my hip until they land on the waistband of my leggings.

He leans over me and whispers in my ear, "Do you want this?"

My mind races with uncertainty and desire. *Do I?* Who am I kidding? The minute he touched me I was his.

"Yes," I reply in a voice that is surprisingly seductive. I didn't know I had that in me.

A jolt of electricity shoots through my body as Omar's hand joins mine. I feel a rush of confidence and any embarrassment is wiped out by the wave of desire for him. This is what I've wanted and it feels like the most natural thing in the world for Omar to take over.

His palm is rough against my skin and he rubs slowly, taking his time as he finds the perfect rhythm to drive me closer to my release. The contrast between my rushed, desperate movements and his deliberate action is startling. It's as if he's savouring every moment, relishing the power he holds over me.

“I want to see you,” I sigh and flick the switch I had trouble finding earlier.

Omar's eyes are fixed on me and the intensity in his gaze sends shivers down my spine. His other hand sneaks under my top to my chest and I feel his fingers gently wrap around my nipple, tugging until they pebble under his touch. I arch my back, pushing my breast into his hand as a low moan escapes my lips. I lie there, unable to think or breathe properly.

"You're so beautiful, Bri," he murmurs, his voice rough with desire. "I’ve been trying not to look at you like that, to keep this professional. I know I shouldn’t be doing it but I’m tired of fighting it. If you want me, tell me and I’m yours."

My heart beats faster at his words. The thought of being desired by Omar sends a wave of heat across my skin. I feel myself getting lost in the moment, surrender creeping in as his expert fingers work their magic.

With a newfound determination, I sit up abruptly, breaking the intense eye contact. The movement causes my shirt to ride up, revealing the curve of my hips. I tuck on the hem of my tank top and pull it over my head. Omar's breath hitches and his eyes darken further as they trail down my body.

I don't give him time to react or object. Leaning in, I capture his lips in a deep, passionate kiss. Our tongues slide against each other and I feel Omar's hunger and desire mix with mine. His hands grasp my waist, pulling me into his lap as if he could merge our bodies into one.

I break the kiss briefly, panting, and whisper, "Don't hold back, Omar. I want this as much as you do."

He groans in response, his hands now roaming freely over my body. I shudder at the feel of his palms against my bare skin when he cups my boobs. His fingers tease my nipples, sending shocks straight to my core and I can't help but grind against his hard cock. *Oh wow, that doesn't feel moderate at all.*

"You're killing me, Bri," he growls, his voice strained with lust. "Seeing you like this, all for me."

The way he says 'all for me' sends a thrill through me and I desperately want to please him, to match the intensity of his desire. As if reading my mind, Omar strips his T-shirt off, his movements eager and clumsy. I roll off him and help him shed his clothes, revelling in the feel of his warm skin against mine as we kiss and explore each other's bodies.

“Naked, now,” he demands as he nibbles on my neck. His fingers push impatiently on the waistband of my leggings and between the two of us we manage to get the tight trousers off me.

I run my hands over his muscular chest, relishing the feel of his firm pecs beneath my palms. A dark trail of hair is leading from the sprinkling of his chest down to a well-groomed savanna.

The thought has me giggling.

“Did you just laugh when looking at my dick?” he asks but there's a mischievous twinkle in his eyes.

“No, I was admiring your well-kept grassland,” I laugh. I really do suck at dirty talk! “Your magnificent cock is nothing to laugh at,” I add my voice laced with desire. My fingers gently circle the tip of his stiff shaft, making Omar hiss.

His lips trail down my jawline and I moan as his hot breath caresses my skin. He nibbles on my ear, his voice low and husky as he asks, "Are you sure about this, Bri? We can't go back once we cross this line."

I nod, unable to speak as the weight of the moment bears down on me. That’s all it takes for him to fully take charge of the situation, and he gently but firmly guides me onto my back. He parts my legs with his knees, and I feel the weight of his body above me as he settles between my thighs.

The anticipation is killing me and I can't wait to feel him inside me. He slowly trails his fingers along my hips down to my mound, and I quiver in anticipation.

With a confident smirk, he slides his fingers lower and slides them through my wetness. “All for me,” he mumbles to himself and the fire in his eyes makes me feel like the most desirable person in the world.

"You're so wet for me, Bri," he breathes, his finger grazing my core. "I can't wait to be inside you. But... I don’t have protection with me."

“I do,” I mumble and scramble from his embrace. I should feel self-conscious as I strut butt naked through the room but I don’t. He made it clear how much he wants me with the desire in his eyes. I fish a few condoms from my handbag and throw them on the bed before rejoining him.

He pulls me into a deep kiss before he unwraps one and rolls it on. I desperately crave his touch and pull him down to me. Lifting my hips I urge him on, needing him to satisfy the fire that's been building between us.

With a smouldering look, he positions himself at my entrance but he's not ready to give me what I want. Grabbing hold of his cock, he slides it up and down my slit coating it in my arousal.

"Ask for it," he demands making me gasp. I can't describe what this dominant side does to me.

"Omar, I need you."

"What do you need?" His eyes are locked on me as he pats my pussy lips with his cock.

"Don't tease me!"

"Say it, Bri. I need to hear you say it." I'm not sure if it's an erotic thing or if he just wants confirmation that I want this, or both, but I'm ready to beg for it.

"Omar, I want you to fuck me. I want you, all of you," I moan.

He places a long kiss on my lips and slowly, so slowly, pushes his tip into me.

"More," I groan and lock my legs behind his arse to pull him closer.

This seems to break whatever has been holding him back and he begins to thrust. I feel stretched and full as he fills me, our eyes lock in an intense stare that speaks volumes. Omar's pace quickens, his powerful thighs driving him into me with force.

The room fills with the wet sounds of our bodies colliding and the occasional low moan escaping my lips. Omar's hands grasp my thighs, leaving marks that will remind me of this night. He leans in, his lips brushing against my ear as he growls, “So good, you feel so good!”

His words almost push me over the edge but I hang on. One of his hands finds a nipple and starts to squeeze. I raise my arms above me and grab the slats of the headboard. I’m so close to the edge. I want to let go and come but at the same time I don’t want it to end.

"Come for me, Bri. Show me how much you've wanted this."

Those words break me and I cry out as my orgasm washes over me. I can't think, can't breathe, as the climax sweeps through me. My back arches and I feel my core pulsate around him.

Omar joins me in ecstasy as the intensity peaks. His roar fills the room and I’m sure the whole B&B knows what we’re doing. We ride out the climax together, our bodies glistening with perspiration, and collapse in a heap, breathless and satisfied.

We lie entangled, catching our breath. The room is filled with just the sounds of our laboured breathing. Omar's arm is draped over me and I savour the feel of his bare skin against mine.

We've crossed a line and the implications settle in as we lie there. This isn't just about tonight—it changes everything between us. I feel it in the way Omar holds me, protectively and possessively.

“Wow,” I finally break the silence.

“Yeah,” he replies quietly and I start to wonder if he’s already regretting it. He gets off the bed without another word and heads to the bathroom; I assume to take care of the condom. I hear the shower turn on before he pokes his head back out of the bathroom.

"Care to join me?" he asks with a grin. Guess that means he doesn't regret it.

Thank fuck for that!

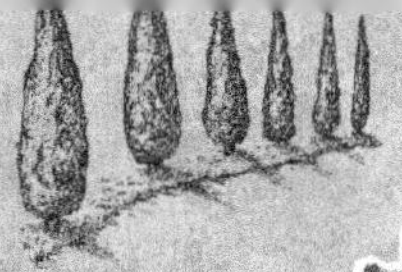

Seventeen

L'accordo

The Agreement

Omar

I carefully carry the tray up the stairs. Cecilia was kind enough to put breakfast together and allow me to take it upstairs. Bri was fast asleep when I snuck out early so I thought I'd surprise her.

After our epic shag, shower and more making out like teenagers, we fell asleep. We didn't really talk but we need to. I don't want to pretend it didn't happen, and we need to clarify what this all means. Was it a one-night thing? Should we have a holiday romance like we talked about in Florence?

I know what I would prefer, but whatever happens I want to make sure we're both on the same page. Despite our conversation at dinner, my attitude towards relationships hasn't changed... I think.

And there's the fact that theoretically I'm her employee, even though it never felt like that because we slipped into friendship mode pretty quickly.

I gently push the door open and find Bri curled up in bed naked, just as I left her half an hour ago. I balance the tray in one hand and close the door with the other before placing the breakfast on the small round table in the centre of the room. I crawl onto the mattress. Bri's face is covered with her hair, so I swipe it away from her neck before placing soft kisses on it. Immediately her taste and scent take over my senses and I have to hold back a groan as all sorts of ideas come to my mind.

"Morning," I whisper when she stirs and keep kissing her. I'm waiting for her to properly wake up, scream at me and declare it was all a mistake. But she doesn't. Instead, she smiles at me and gently cups my face.

"Morning," she grins. I take this as an invite to kiss her again but as I lower myself, she stops me with her hand on my chest.

"I haven't brushed my teeth," she protests.

"I don't give a fuck," I whisper and place a passionate kiss on her lips anyway. She laughs, rolls away from me and slips her tank top and leggings on.

"I brought you breakfast." I point to the table.

"Oh my God. You're my hero," she groans before rushing to the bathroom.

"Hurry up, Snaily. I'll eat all of your beloved croissants."

"You wouldn't dare," she shouts through a mouthful of toothpaste. I really wouldn't dare. I think she'd murder me if I came between her and her favourite pastry. I place one on a plate and put it next to the cup of tea.

"Are you taking the car to the mechanic this morning?" she asks.

"Nope, don't have to. Cecilia said she spoke with the guy and he's willing to come over and have a look here before deciding what to do." Bri nods but doesn't say anything else. She drops into the chair and takes a bite of her croissant.

"Bri... do we need to talk about last night?" I ask carefully. "Actually, *I* want to talk about last night," I clarify.

"Do you think it was a mistake?" she says, her face full of worry.

"Truth be told, I probably should but I don't."

A small smile appears on her lips. "Neither do I... it was just right. I mean, you said it yourself, if I want to have a holiday romance, it should be with someone I can trust who takes care of me, someone who isn't just after a blowie for his bush-dick. Someone who makes me feel special. And you tick all these boxes."

"So you want us to have a holiday romance?" I ask carefully. My heart is hammering.

"Why not? "

"There's the small matter that I'm employed by you. I don't want you to feel like I take advantage of you."

"You're employed by Ben, and if anything I'd be the one taking advantage of you," she laughs.

"Not sure he'd see it the same way."

"Guess what, we don't have to tell him." Bri gets up from her chair and hops onto my lap, linking her arms behind my neck. "Look, I don't see you as my driver, I already think of you as my friend. Neither of us is looking for a relationship but we both clearly could enjoy a holiday romance. I'm not a woman to beg, so if you don't want to or think it's weird, then let's forget about it but let me assure you, I'm serious when I say, I want this." She's about to jump off my lap but I hold her back and pull her into a kiss.

"What happens in Europe stays in Europe?" I ask.

"Technically the UK is still part of Europe but what happens on the continent stays on the continent," she laughs and places a quick kiss on the tip of my nose.

"And once we get to back to England, it's over?"

"Yes."

"Okay, just a holiday romance." I like that idea. I like that idea a lot... I think "No commitment, just a few weeks of fun."

"Fun and sex and amazing kisses," she laughs.

"Oh. Amazing kisses but not amazing sex."

"I've had quite a lot of kisses by now but sex only once. So I think I need to do a little bit more research before I can give you a grade on that," she smirks. *That little minx.*

I lift her up and toss her onto the mattress. She squeals.

"Well, let me prove to you how amazing it is."

"No, Mister, you need to take care of the car and I want a shower," she slides from my grasp, kisses me one last time and walks off to the bathroom. I watch her leave the room and feel happy. But there's also a dark cloud looming in the back of my mind and I can't shake it.

♥

This is what you get when you come to Italy in November. The rain is relentless and we run the last few steps back to the B&B. The mechanic had to take the car to the garage so we're spending a few more nights in Castiglioncello. We walked down into the village for dinner and got caught by the rain on our way back.

We're soaking wet by the time we get back to the room. I peel my T-shirt off and throw it into the bathroom so it doesn't drip all over the floor. As I turn, Bri just stands there and waits for me to slow down and take her in. When she has my attention, she slowly starts to unbutton her blouse.

The soft glow from the lamp on the bedside table illuminates her every move, and her rain-soaked clothes cling to her figure. I take in her every action; the way her eyes flutter as she unbuttons her shirt, revealing a hint of lacy bra beneath. I swallow hard, my mouth going dry at the sight of her slender fingers working on the fastening of her jeans.

I stride forward, my eyes never leaving hers as I reach behind her, unclipping her bra and letting it fall to the floor. Bri's breath hitches and she sighs as my large hands cover her tits, thumbing the taut peaks.

"You have no idea what you do to me," I murmur, my voice rough with desire. I trace the outline of her ear with my tongue and Bri shivers, her hands gripping my upper arms as my lips trail down her neck.

"Let's warm up," I whisper and drag her to the bathroom. I strip off the rest of my clothes and Bri does the same. The shower runs invitingly hot and I step in, pulling Bri with me.

My hands go to work immediately, diligently lathering and exploring every curve of her body, whilst my lips devoured her mouth in deep kisses. Bri's hands roam just as eagerly, exploring me, running up and down my spine, and grasping my bum cheeks.

Bri sighs as I lift her against the shower wall, thrusting my hard cock against her pussy lips. The water splashes against our bodies and Bri's eyes drift close as my hips snap against hers.

"I want to hear you, Bri," I demand, my voice has a rough edge to it. "Scream for me, let the whole place know what we're doing."

Bri's fingers dig into my shoulders as she finds her voice, a lust-filled moan escaping her lips. "Oh God, Omar... I need more! I need you so bad."

Her words almost make me lose control and it takes everything in me to not slip my dick into her warm core.

“No condom, Bri. But there’s something else I can do for you.” I grin and place her back down before sinking to my knees. My lips wander over her stomach down to her mound and over her trimmed hair, looking darker now it’s wet.

I run my fingers through it and make it stand up.

“What are you doing?” she laughs.

“Making a little mohawk.”

“Omar!” She laughs out loud before sliding her fingers over my head and tightly griping my hair. I know what she wants.

I cup the back of her knee and lift one of her legs to rest over my shoulder, giving me access to her clit.

Her moans fill the steamy air as my tongue glides along her slick folds. I'm on my knees, water cascading over both of us, and my focus is entirely on her pleasure.

Her hands are in my hair, urging me closer. I can feel heat radiating from between her thighs, and it fuels my desire to make her come undone. My tongue dips inside her, flicking against her sensitive flesh and making her gasp.

"Fuck," she breathes, her hips pressing forward. I grip onto the curve of her ass, keeping her steady as I devour her with an intensity born from pure hunger.

Her scent is everywhere—sweet and musky—and I know I'll never forget it. I drag my tongue up to circle around her clit, applying just enough pressure to elicit a shudder.

"Right there," she pants, the need in her voice like an aphrodisiac. "Don't stop."

I'm lost in this moment, focused solely on the taste of her against my lips. The water pounds down around us and it feels like we're in our own little world.

Curling two fingers inside of her, I find the spot that drives her wild. Her body jolts with pleasure and a low moan rumbles from deep within. It's music to my ears.

My mouth never stops its attention on her clit—licking, sucking, driving waves of pleasure through every nerve ending. The heat is building between us—her body coiling tight with anticipation—and I know she's close.

I increase the pace of my tongue against her swollen bud and pump my fingers deeper inside her. And then it happens.

She cries out my name as her body shudders and clenches around my fingers. Her juices flow, mixing with the water, and I drink up every drop.

Her legs tremble as I slowly ease off the pressure, savouring the aftershocks that ripple through her. I look up at her, water streaming down my face, and there's a mix of desire and longing in her eyes.

I stand up and claim her lips in a searing kiss.

"Your turn," she breathes out against my mouth, her hands trailing down my chest to grip onto my hardening cock.

“Bri, that’s not a good idea. I want to come in—” My words are cut short when she swipes with her thumb over the tip of my dick.

I groan at the touch, overwhelmed by sensation, and let her guide me to where she wants me. She positions me under the spray, then pushes me back until I'm leaning against the cold tile wall.

Her hand wraps around my length—hot and slick—and begins to stroke me in a slow rhythm that drives me to the edge. My head falls back against the tiles and a low growl escapes from deep within me.

She cups my balls with her free hand and massages them gently which adds an extra layer of intensity that has me teetering on the edge.

"Stop, please," I grunt as she increases her pace, bringing me closer and closer to that precipice of release. “Bri!” I grab hold of her hand, “Bedroom, now!”

I wrap her in a towel before guiding her out of the bathroom. She drops the towel and crawls on the mattress, giving me a perfect view of her amazing round arse. *Who can resist her? Not me!* I lie down next to her, the coolness of the linen sheets contrasting with the heat of our bodies, sending shivers down my spine.

I don’t give Bri time to ponder as I crawl on top of her, my lips attacking hers in a passionate kiss. Our tongues slide against each other, exploring and enticing.

"You're so sexy, Omar," Bri whispers, her voice breathless. "I need you now, right this minute.”

I reach for the nightstand and grab a condom. Bri pulls it from my fingers and rolls it onto my throbbing cock. It’s almost painful to let her touch me because I’m so on edge.

I glance down at her, seeking confirmation, and find myself lost in her gaze. With a deep, satisfying groan I slide into her, my eyes never leaving Bri's as I fill her completely.

Bri's hands grip the duvet even tighter, her back arching off the bed in response to my deliberate thrusts. I set a steady rhythm that feels so good that I wish it could go on forever. The bed creaks loudly in time with our movements, but I couldn’t care less if the whole village hears us.

"Harder," Bri demands. "I want you as close as you can be to me." I capture her mouth in a deep kiss whilst giving her exactly what asked for. Her nails dig into my back and she lifts her hips to meet me at every stroke.

"You're so perfect, Bri."

At my words Bri's climax sweeps over her and I feel the convulsions of her body around me. I pump into her a few more times before releasing a primal roar and collapsing on top of her. For a second, I forget to breathe and my senses are filled with her and her alone.

"That was... I can confirm sex with you is also amazing," Bri sighs, her body relaxed and sated underneath me. "I've never experienced anything like that."

I prop myself up on my arms. "You're amazing," I reply. "You are one. Amazing. Woman."

Bri cups my cheeks again, a gesture that fills me with warmth every time she does it. Our lips meet in a tender kiss filling in the gaps left by the words we don't dare say.

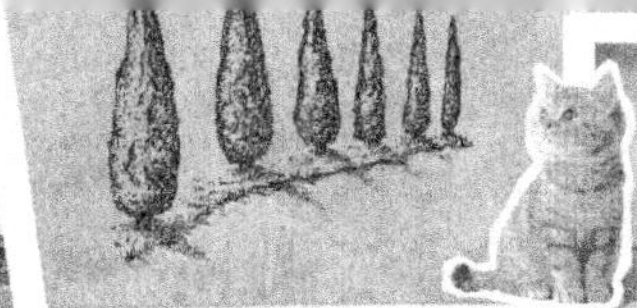

Eighteen

La nuova me

The New Me

Bridget

THE SPOON CLINKS SOFTLY against the glass bowl as I take another bite of gelato. I'd choose ice cream, especially Italian ice cream, over hot chocolate any day, even in November when it's cold enough outside to see your breath. There's something about the way it melts on your tongue—creamy, sweet, a little escape from everything. I sit back in my chair, watching bundled-up people hurry by on the cobblestone street outside. For once I'm not rushing anywhere. No one asking me for anything. It's just me, this cosy café, and my gelato.

My phone buzzes, shattering my little bubble. I glance at the screen—Ruthie. I sigh, swipe to answer, and press the phone to my ear. "Hey, darling."

"Mum, oh my God, you'll never guess what happened today!"

Here we go. I settle back in my chair, take another bite of gelato, and prepare for the onslaught. "What happened?"

"So, I'm in this lecture and Professor Henderson tells the whole class that my essay was superb."

"That's great, darling." I swirl my spoon around in the gelato, watching it melt a bit, and half-listen as she rattles on about her essay and how stressful her master's programme is.

"And, guess what, oh you'll never guess, after the class, she asked me to stay behind and invited me to be part of a project she's doing. Can you believe it? If I impress her doing that she could support my PhD application after my masters."

"That's wonderful Ruthie! I'm so proud of you!" I'm always proud of my children but she's incredible at her studies. She has determination that Christopher never had and if she wants something she makes it happen.

The bell above the café door jingles and I glance up just in time to see Omar stroll in, hands in his jacket pockets, scanning the tables until he spots me. A grin tugs at the corner of his lips and I feel an instant flutter in my stomach—one that still surprises me, even now.

"Ruthie, love, I've got to—" I start to say, but she barrels right on.

"Anyway, I'm a bit nervous though. What if I cock it up? She normally only invites PhD students to take part in her projects"

Omar slides into the seat across from me, nodding at my gelato. "You saving some for me?" he whispers, a mischievous look in his eye.

I swat him away with my free hand, and mouth, "Ruthie." He grins and leans back in his chair, clearly amused.

"She wouldn't have asked you if she didn't believe you could do it," I say to Ruthie, my eyes still on Omar as he steals a spoonful of my gelato.

"You really think so?" Ruthie asks. "I don't know, I think I'm nervous. Maybe it's silly."

"You'll be fine, Ruthie. I know you can do it," I say, but my focus is split between her and Omar, who's now making a show of dramatically savouring the ice cream. I give him a mock glare, but he just winks.

"Mum, am I interrupting something?" Ruthie's voice pulls me back.

I straighten up, trying to cover that Omar is distracting me. "Of course not, I'm listening! I'm just... multitasking."

Ruthie laughs. "Alright, I'll let you go. You're probably busy enjoying yourself over there in Italy. I'll call you later, okay? Love you!"

"Love you too, sweetheart," I say before she hangs up. I drop the phone on the table and give Omar a look. "You're a terrible influence."

He leans forward, spoon still in hand, and raises an eyebrow. "I'm not the one ignoring my daughter."

"I'm not ignoring her. It's just difficult to explain why I'm distracted," I say, snatching the spoon from him and taking a triumphant bite. "Not that she really asked. She wasn't even interested in how the trip is going. Sometimes it feels like my children think my whole existence is limited to *being Mum*. Ruthie had some fantastic news to share, but would it be too much to just ask how I am?"

"Sounds about right." Omar chuckles, leaning back. "She's twenty-two. Isn't that prime 'self-involved' age?"

I can't help but laugh. "Maybe I'm just being selfish. Of course she'd want to tell me her good news."

"When we are young we forget that our parents also have lives. I think in our minds they just sit at home and do fuck all because their lives are over." Omar grins, and I laugh again.

"Probably," I say, shaking my head. "But this trip... it's the first time I haven't been at their beck and call. The first time I've been able to focus on what I want."

"And what's that?" Omar asks, his voice dropping a little, a hint of something playful but serious in his eyes.

I raise an eyebrow. "Gelato. Lots of it."

He chuckles. "Fair enough. But seriously. This trip, it's done something to you. I've only known you for a short time but even I can see the change."

I pause with my spoon halfway to my mouth and realise he's right. I feel different. I've felt it since we started travelling together, but I hadn't really put it into words. "I think... I think I just forgot what it was like to live for myself. To not have to worry about the kids or my job or what my ex thinks I'm doing wrong."

Omar nods, leaning forward on his elbows. "It suits you, you know. This version of you."

I look at him, taken aback for a moment. "What version is that?"

"The one that's not trying to be everything for everyone else. The one that's just... you."

I feel warmth spread through me but I try to deflect the compliment with a little laugh. "Well I don't know about that. I'm still me. Still dealing with Ruthie's dramas. But, yeah, I suppose... I do feel different here. It's like I've been carrying everyone else's stuff for so long, I forgot what it's like to just carry my own."

"You're allowed to do that, you know," Omar says, his voice softer now. "Put yourself first."

I look at him and we sit in comfortable silence for a moment, the world outside the café feeling a million miles away. He's right, of course. But it's easier said than done. "I'm not used to it. I've always been the fixer. The responsible one. You should've seen me with the kids when they were little. It was non-stop—one scrape, one tantrum after the other."

"And now they're grown. You don't have to do that anymore."

"I know," I say, though it's more to myself than to him. "I think this is the first time I've really allowed myself to believe it."

Omar reaches across the table and nudges the gelato towards me. "While you're believing in yourself, you can have the rest of this."

I narrow my eyes, pretending to be suspicious. "You sure you're not just trying to offload your calories onto me?"

"I would never," he says with a mock-serious expression.

I laugh and take another bite, feeling lighter than I've in a long time. "Thanks for that, by the way."

"For what?"

"For reminding me I'm allowed to enjoy my own life."

He grins. "Any time."

I lean back in my chair, taking in the atmosphere of the café, the quiet clinking of dishes, the comfortable silence between us. For the first time in years I'm not thinking about what anyone else needs. Not Ruthie, not Christopher, not my boss, not my ex.

Just me. And, well... maybe Omar, too.

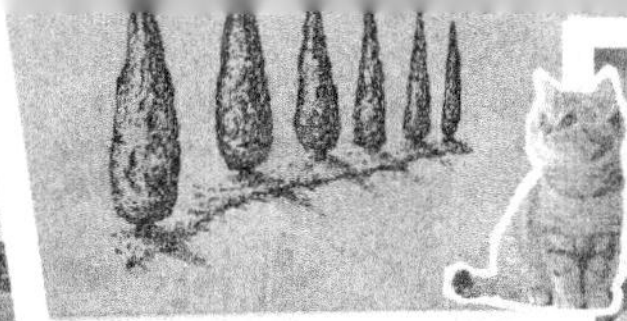

Nineteen

Il colosseo

The Collosseum

Bridget

ROME IN NOVEMBER HAS a certain charm to it. The streets are quiet, the air is crisp, and the sun's just warm enough to keep the chill at bay. Omar and I are wrapped up in jackets; he is wearing one of these sporty beanies and I have a thick scarf wrapped around me. We are walking side by side, our breath puffing out in little clouds; we look like one of these autumn vibe social media posts. Despite the cooler weather the city still buzzes with life, scooters weaving through the narrow streets and tourists snapping photos of everything they see.

"Bloody hell, it's massive," I say, staring up at the ancient stone walls of the Colosseum. The pictures don't do it justice—it's even more impressive in person. "Do you think we're allowed to take bits of it home as souvenirs?"

Omar chuckles next to me. "Yeah, sure, I'll just stick a chunk in my rucksack and hope no one notices."

I elbow him lightly. "Come on, it's not like they're using all of it anymore."

"Right. You, me, and a brick from the Colosseum... and a fine from the Carabinieri. Perfect holiday memory." He smirks, glancing down at me. "Want me to grab some cobblestones while I'm at it?"

I grin. "Tempting but I'll pass. I've already stubbed my toe on one, and that's enough of a memory. And I'm pretty sure the police here have better things to do than to fine us."

Omar, the know-it-all, pulls his phone out of his pocket, types something and then holds out an article about an American who was fined twenty thousand Euros for stealing a piece of the Colosseum.

"Still want a souvenir?" he smirks.

"I would have believed you without Google." I stick my tongue out at him and he shakes his head, laughing.

We head towards the entrance, our shoes echoing on the uneven stones beneath our feet. I'm glad I didn't go for sandals in this weather—my trusty trainers are doing the job just fine. The cold air nips at my cheeks but the excitement of being here keeps me warm. I glance over at Omar, who's looking ridiculously good in his sports jacket and cargo trousers, like he's stepped out of a bloody GQ ad.

"Stop staring," he says without looking at me, a smirk tugging at the corner of his lips.

I scoff. "I'm not staring. I'm just... appreciating the architecture."

"Right," he says, raising an eyebrow, "and which part of the Colosseum is my face again?"

"'The part that's falling apart but still looks good from a distance," I shoot back.

A deep belly laugh erupts from Omar. "Cheeky."

As we step inside the Colosseum the world seems to shift. The sounds of the city fade, replaced by the quiet hum of history. Knowing that so many people once stood where we're standing now, watching gladiators fight, crowds cheering is strange. It feels... surreal.

"This place is incredible," I whisper, my voice echoing slightly in the stone corridors.

"Not bad," Omar says, glancing around. "Could use a bit of patching up though. Maybe some central heating."

I laugh, the sound bouncing off the ancient walls. "Yeah, I'm sure they're just waiting for the right builder."

We wander along the corridor, the crisp November air following us through the open archways. It's quieter than I expected which makes it feel more intimate, like we've stumbled upon a hidden secret. Every now and then our hands brush, and each time it sends a little jolt through me like I'm suddenly hyper-aware of how close we are. When we're in the bedroom together we're insatiable, but when we're out in the city we're flirty and shy like a couple on their first date, and I don't know which part of this I lov—enjoy more.

We stop in front of the open arena, looking down at the ruins below. Omar pulls me closer, his arm slipping around my waist. I glance up at him and he's already looking at me, his dark eyes soft and warm.

"You cold?" he asks, his voice low.

I shake my head, though my cheeks feel a little flushed and not from the weather. "Nope. No, on the contrary."

His lips quirk into a half-smile and I can see a teasing glint in his eyes. "Good. Can't have you freezing to death in the middle of the Colosseum."

"Very heroic of you," I say, leaning into him. "Saving me from a Roman winter."

He chuckles, the sound rumbling through his chest. "Someone's got to do it."

We stand there for a moment just enjoying the view, the autumn air, the closeness. I tilt my head up just as Omar's leaning down, his face just inches from mine. I feel my heart pick up pace, my pulse quickening as his lips hover near mine.

He gently brushes a piece of hair away from my face, his fingers lingering on my skin, and I feel the heat rising in my chest despite the cool air around us. His eyes flick to my lips, and just like that, everything else falls away—the tourists, the cold, the Colosseum itself.

He leans in, and as his lips touch mine it's like the world stops. The kiss is soft and slow, the kind that makes your knees feel a bit wobbly and your head a little light. I lean into him, my hands resting on his chest, feeling the steady beat of his heart.

When he pulls back his forehead rests against mine, and I can't help but smile.

"Definitely the best way to explore Roman history ever," I murmur.

Omar grins, his thumb brushing my cheek. "Got to make it memorable, right?"

"You're doing a decent job of it," I admit with a cheeky smile.

We spend the next hour wandering around the Colosseum, snapping pictures, sneaking in a few more kisses, and laughing at how ridiculous we look in the photos. Omar keeps trying to act all serious but he cracks every time I pull a face.

"Come on, act like a gladiator!" I tease, holding up my phone for another shot.

Omar crosses his arms, narrowing his eyes in a mock-serious expression. "Is that what you wanted?"

"Perfect," I laugh, snapping the picture. "You look terrifying."

"Good," he says with a smirk. "That's the goal."

The sun's beginning to dip as we leave the Colosseum, casting a golden glow over the square. I spot a group of fake Roman soldiers standing by the entrance, fully decked out in costumes, helmets gleaming in the fading light.

"Ooh, Omar, look!" I say, grabbing his arm. "We've got to get a picture with them."

He rolls his eyes. "Really? You want a photo with those guys? I'm pretty sure it's illegal for them to be there taking money of tourists."

"Who's talking about money? Look, there's tons of them. Must be some event or something. Come on."

"I'm not sure—"

"But I am," I say, dragging him towards the nearest soldier. "It's Rome, you've got to embrace the tourist stuff."

The soldier flashes me a grin as I approach. "Ah, bella! You want a picture with a real Roman?"

I laugh. "Real Roman, sure. Let's do it."

I hand Omar my phone, and he sighs dramatically as he lines up the shot. "Alright, let's make this quick."

The soldier puts his arm around me, striking a dramatic pose with his fake sword. "Say 'Caesar'!"

"Caesar!" I giggle, and just as Omar snaps the picture, the soldier leans in and plants a cheeky kiss on my cheek.

I blink, surprised, and burst out laughing. "Oi! No one said anything about kisses!" I had an encounter with an Italian stallion and I think I stick to British-Lebanese men for now.

The soldier just winks at me. "When in Rome, bella." I wave at them as they walk off towards a larger group of fake soldiers. I should have asked them what the event was.

I head over to Omar, who's standing with the phone in his hand, his jaw tight. I take the mobile from him, glancing at the picture. "We look brilliant!"

"Yeah, fantastic," he mutters, not even glancing at the photo. His hands are shoved in his pockets and his expression is tense.

I nudge him playfully. "What's up with you? You jealous of the fake Roman soldier?"

He scoffs, though it's clear he's trying to hide his annoyance.

I raise an eyebrow, grinning. "Oh, come on. You are!"

He sighs, running a hand through his hair. "Alright, fine. Maybe a little."

I laugh, slipping my arms around his waist. "Omar, I'm pretty sure I'm not the first tourist he's kissed. He probably does it a hundred times a day."

"Yeah well, I still didn't like it," he grumbles, though I can see the corner of his mouth twitching.

I lean up, kissing his jaw. "You know you're the only one I want kissing me, right?"

His arms wrap around me, pulling me close. "I better be."

I grin up at him. "Want me to prove it?"

He laughs, shaking his head, but leans down and kisses me anyway, this time not holding back. When we finally pull apart, I'm breathless.

"There," he says with a smirk.

"I thought I was supposed to prove it to you?" I laugh as we start walking again, hand in hand. I get butterflies when his fingers lock with mine. *Is that normal for holiday flings?*

"Next stop?" Omar asks, glancing at me.

I think for a second. "Pizza. Obviously."

"Obviously," he agrees with a grin.

We stroll through the Roman streets, the Colosseum fading behind us, and I can't help but think that despite the cheeky Roman soldier, it's been the perfect day. And with pizza on the way it's about to get even better.

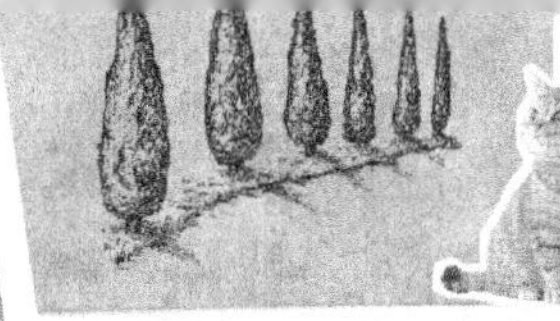

Twenty

I gatti

The Cats

Omar

ROME IS SPECIAL. IT'S always been my number one city in the world, beating Beirut to second place. But turns out exploring Rome with an amazing person like Bri takes it to another level.

We finally got the car back three days ago, although the mechanic warned us that he couldn't guarantee how long the Beast will last. As much as we enjoyed Castiglioncello, we left on the same day for Rome and have been exploring the city ever since.

Of course, we did our hop-on-hop-off bus tour but we also went to see the Vatican and the Colosseum where I actually got jealous of a bloody gladiator because Bri let him kiss her on the cheek.

Yesterday we sat on one of the benches above circus Maximus for two hours, and just soaked up the amazing view of the Palatino and talked about everything and nothing. She told me about her children, her divorce. I told her about my childhood and my time with my family in the Middle East. We spoke about our dreams and hopes. I love that she's considering going back to university. I'm proof that it's never too late to change your career.

Bri's easy to talk to and even easier to tease. She doesn't mind laughing at herself. She has a serious side and intelligent side and a funny side. When all three come together, she's the most marvellous person I've ever met and it's already making me feel anxious about the end of our holiday romance. Sometimes I catch myself wondering what if, but then I remind myself that the divorce rate is forty-two percent and nothing lasts forever, especially not a holiday romance. *Let's stay realistic here.*

Today I'm taking her to the Cat Ladies of Rome. I haven't told her where we're off to but I promised her she'll love it.

"Are you going to tell me where we're going?" she asks again as we get off the bus. Largo di Torre Argentina is a lively square filled with ancient ruins. The road surrounding it is busy with traffic and people. Fenced off in the centre are four old temples and the remains of Curia di Pompea where Julius Caesar was assassinated. But we're not here to see the ruins, strictly speaking. At the far end of the ancient buildings steps lead down to a lower level and this is where I drag Bri.

As we turn the corner she throws a glimpse down into the ruins and squeals.

"Oh my God. Look, there's a cat." She points at a little ginger who lies curled up in a flower pot, snoozing in the sun. As we walk closer I point at a sign: Cat Ladies of

Rome. The ancient ruins are home to a large number of cats who are taken care of by a group of volunteers.

"What is this place?" she asks, more to herself than to me, before hopping down the stairs to the entrance. Whilst the cats roam freely they also have a safe place to sleep where they get fed. They're more like pets with ancient ruins for a playground.

Bri's in her element. She moves from cat to cat, cooing over each furball. When she starts chatting with one of the volunteers I'm roped in as a translator and can barely keep up with the two very excited women chatting about their cats. Bri fishes out her phone and shows the lady a photo of Bella and they have another round of multilingual chitchat.

I think bringing her here was the right thing. I'm never going to understand her fascination with cats; I don't mind them, but I don't really need them in my life. But Bri, she clearly is a cat lady. And giving her this experience and seeing her excitement, makes me happy.

"What now?" Bri asks when I finally manage to get her away from the cats, almost two hours after we arrived.

"Hmm. I was thinking, how about a little break in our room?" I wink.

"Omar, we're in Rome."

"Yeah, and when in Rome, do like the Romans do?" I wiggle my eyebrows to make it very clear what I plan to do to her in our bedroom.

"What would make you think they're shagging in the afternoon?" she giggles.

"Well—"

"I don't think so." She shakes her head but cuddles up in my arms all the same.

"Come on. Let's have a break and then we can go to the Foro Traiano and see the light show in the evening."

"Fine. But just a nap." She gives me a triumphant smirk but we'll see who wins this round. We've been at it like bunnies since we slept together the first time so I'm pretty sure it won't take long for us to explore each other's bodies once we hit the mattress. She's nothing like any woman I've met before. Maybe it's because she's a bit older than me, and I usually go for women in their early thirties. But Bri, she's different. She knows exactly what she wants, and she's not shy about going after it. She's confident in a way that draws me in. It's not just about sex with her; it's something more. She enjoys it, sure, but it's not the kind of quick, casual thing you could have with anyone. When we're together, it's like she pulls me into this intimate, almost otherworldly experience. The connection is intense, and I can't remember ever feeling that way before with anyone else.

By the time we get back to the hotel the idea of a nap feels like the best thing ever. We've been up since five this morning, having dragged ourselves out of bed to see the Fontana di Trevi at sunrise before the crowds descended. It was worth it because it was almost empty, just us and the fountain. We got some beautiful photos, and of course we threw a coin in.

Bri wanted to throw in a second and even a third. I had to stop her. Call me superstitious, but the whole "three coins means you'll marry an Italian" legend? Yeah, I don't need her to fall victim to another Italian stallion. We had a bit of a back-and-forth about it—Bri thought the three coins thing was a romantic myth, and I tried my hardest to convince her that it's just a silly movie reference. I don't need to tempt fate like that. I know it's ridiculous but I couldn't help myself. Better safe than sorry.

When we finally make it to our room we collapse onto the bed like we've just finished a marathon. Bri curls up in my arms and I swear it feels so good it almost hurts. Her head rests on my chest, and she traces lazy circles on my stomach with her finger, like it's the most natural thing in the world.

"I've been thinking," she murmurs, her voice soft but clear. "Maybe we should move on tomorrow. Perugia for a night or two, then San Marino. We're running out of time and I want to make sure we get to Padua before heading to Salzburg."

I feel my chest tighten. Not because of the places she's rattling off, but because of what she's really saying: we're running out of time. There are only a few cities left to see and then this trip will be over. And so will our arrangement.

"Sounds good," I say, keeping my voice steady but I can feel the dread settling in, heavy and thick. I don't want to talk about it. I don't want to think about what happens when this trip is over. Although we had both agreed to it, the thought of her going back to her life and me to mine nothing has ever sounded more unappealing. But I don't want to spoil this moment.

She keeps drawing circles on my stomach, her touch light and soothing, and I just lie there staring at the ceiling, trying to ignore the knot in my chest. I love how easy this all feels—her in my arms, the quiet between us. It's the kind of comfort you don't find with just anyone. *Stop it, Omar! Get a grip. This is not you.*

"We'll still make it to all the places you want," I say, trying to sound casual. "Plenty of time." It's technically not quite true because we have to leave Salzburg by the twenty ninth of November to make it back on the thirtieth, a day ahead of the wedding party. That leaves us exactly nine days.

Bri tilts her head up, her eyes meeting mine. "You're not... dreading the end of the trip, are you?"

I feel my stomach flip. She's asking the question I've been dodging in my head for days. I want to tell her the truth—that I'm dreading it like hell. But I shrug instead, trying to play it off. "A bit. You?"

She gives a half-smile that doesn't quite reach her eyes. "Yeah... it's been amazing, hasn't it?"

"Yeah," I say, pulling her a little closer. "It has."

We lie in silence for a while with the weight of what's unspoken hanging between us. I now know why it's so different with Bri. She became a friend first. She was relentless in making sure we get to know each other for the first couple of weeks, asking me lots of questions and making sure I heard every hilarious story from her life. She's true to herself, what you see is what you get. She doesn't play games, she doesn't pretend to be someone cleverer, sexier, more sophisticated. She's just who she is and she's adorable. And only once we were friends, we explored this other side, opened us up to more.

I try to banish the thought that maybe this all was a big mistake from my mind. Every cell in me is screaming that this will end in heartache but I ignore them. Instead, I focus on the feel of her body curled against mine, her soft breath against my chest. I don't want to ruin these last days by giving in to my inner alarm bells.

"Let's not think about it now," I say finally, my voice quiet. "We've still got time."

She nods against my chest, her finger still tracing those circles. I press my lips to hers, soft at first, then with more urgency. Her mouth opens for me, our tongues dancing as my hands explore her body. She's so fucking beautiful. Every inch of her is a masterpiece.

Her perfect tits are in my hands, the perky nipples hardening under my touch. I need to taste her. I push her T-Shirt up and lower my mouth to her chest, sucking on each nipple through her bra until she moans beneath me.

Her fingers are in my hair, tugging gently, urging me downwards. I kiss a trail down her stomach, stopping briefly to swirl my tongue around her belly button. She laughs and squirms beneath me.

I deliberately take my time unbuttoning her jeans and pulling them off.

"You need to get naked too," she commands. I give her a wink and crawl of the bed. I reach behind me and pull my shirt off.

"More?" I ask with a smirk.

"Trousers off, Mister," she orders. I slowly unbutton my jeans and push them down a few inches before pulling them back up like I'm a bloody stripper. Bri loves it. She giggles excitedly and wolf whistles.

When I slowly start to push my jeans down again her fingers land on her clit and she starts to circle it. *Fuck that's hot.*

"If you don't hurry up, Snaily", she uses my nickname for her, "I'll do it myself."

I lose my trousers and boxer shorts in one go and join her on the bed, swatting her fingers aside and lowering my head until I reach the prize between her legs. I can smell how wet she is—the intoxicating scent of arousal that drives me wild every time.

I push her knickers aside and my tongue finds her clit. I circle it slowly before flicking it back and forth. She bucks against me, gripping the bedsheet as pleasure courses through her body.

I slip two fingers inside her pussy, curling them upwards to reach that special spot that makes her scream my name. Her hips move with mine as I fuck her with my hand and devour her clit with my mouth.

I can tell she's close now by the way she's writhing beneath me, moaning my name over and over again like a prayer.

I increase the speed of my hand and tongue until she's on the edge of release, then push her right over it.

She comes hard against me, thighs clamping around my head as she rides out the waves of pleasure crashing through her body. *Fuck, she tastes good.*

I kiss my way back up and lock eyes with Bri as she catches her breath. She pulls me into a passionate kiss, tasting herself on my lips.

"Fuck me," she whispers against my mouth and I don't need telling twice.

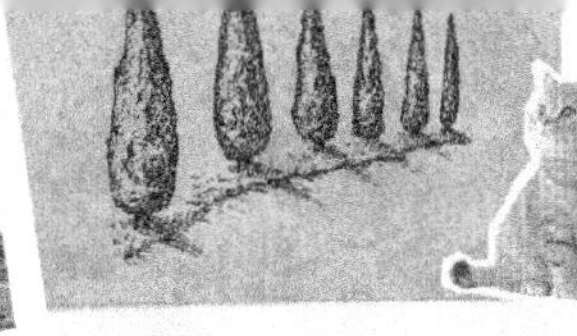

Twenty-One

La zucca

The Pumpkin

Bridget

OMAR'S LIPS PRESS SOFTLY against mine and I melt into the kiss. The taste of his mouth, the warmth of his body, all consuming. We're in Rome and it feels like a dream, somewhere far from our everyday lives.

I run my fingers through his hair as his hands explore my body, pulling me closer to him. The world outside these four walls fades away and it's just us. His touch is electric, sending shivers down my spine. Every nerve ending is on fire.

He breaks away from the kiss and looks at me with those intense dark eyes that make me weak at the knees.

"I want you," he whispers, his voice thick with desire.

My heart pounds in my chest as I nod, unable to find the words to express how much I want him too.

He's hard and ready for me and it's like a drug. In this moment I need him more than anything. He rolls on a condom and enters me slowly, inch by inch, until he's completely inside me. We both moan at the sensation; it doesn't matter how often we do this, it always feels perfect.

He starts to move with slow and deep thrusts. Every movement sends waves of pleasure crashing through me. It feels like we're two bodies becoming one; nothing else matters.

We move together in perfect rhythm as we chase that sweet release. His hands are on my hips, pulling me closer with each thrust. Our eyes lock and I see something in his gaze that is overwhelming.

I can feel pressure building inside me, getting stronger with every stroke. It's like a tidal wave about to crash over us and I never want it to end.

I reach down between us and start to touch myself, adding another layer of intensity to the already electric air. His eyes never leave mine as I bring myself closer to the edge.

I'm so close when he takes over, his fingers expertly finding exactly what I need.

That's all it takes; the dam breaks and the orgasm spreads through me like wildfire. My back arches off the bed as I ride it out.

I can feel him getting close too; his thrusts are faster now, more urgent. He lets go completely and joins me in that euphoric release with one final push.

We collapse onto the bed, completely spent. He wraps his arms around me and pulls me into him, holding me tightly. I can hear his heart beating in time with mine and it's the most comforting sound.

We lay there in silence for a while, basking in the afterglow. It's a moment I never want to end. But eventually reality starts to seep back in and we know we have to leave this haven we've created. *It's not over yet, we have nine more days.* Somehow this doesn't feel as much of a comfort as it should.

This place is absolutely charming. We've really lucked out with the weather too and Perugia is a picture-perfect little Italian village. The roads are steep but despite that we've been up and down them so many times now and I think I'm falling for this place. It's just so cute.

"The food was incredible," I say, trying to catch my breath. The street leading back to the hotel is especially steep and I'm a bit winded.

"It really was. I had serious food envy when I saw your Carbonara," Omar laughs, his voice light. The restaurant was quite posh with a menu to match. I had Carbonara parcels—basically, little pasta pillows filled with delicious Carbonara sauce, sitting on a sprinkle of crispy bacon and drizzled with basil oil. I shared one with Omar but the rest were all mine.

I'm about to reply when I hear a faint squeak.

"What was that?" I ask, pausing in my tracks.

"What?" Omar looks at me, puzzled.

"Didn't you hear that?"

"No." He shakes his head, looking around.

"Listen." We stand in silence but there's nothing. Maybe I imagined it. But just as we start walking again I hear it—a soft squeak.

"That sounds more like... meowing!" I say, suddenly excited. We both start scanning the area—under cars, in flower pots—until I spot it: two tiny, sparkling eyes peeking out from under a red Fiat.

"Come here, kitty, kitty, kitty," I coax, making little smacking noises with my lips. "Try calling it in Italian," I suggest.

"I don't think cats care whether you speak Italian or English."

I shoot Omar a mock glare and continue trying to coax the kitten out. It's hesitant but eventually, a teeny tiny ginger kitten cautiously emerges. As I pick him up I realise he's just a baby, too young to be out here alone. He lets out a pitiful cry and I feel him shivering in the cold wind. Without thinking I quickly unzip my jacket and tuck him inside, where he snuggles against my warm chest.

"There must be a mother cat around here somewhere," Omar says, scanning the area again. But after searching and even ringing a few doorbells we come up empty. No one seems to be missing a kitten.

"What are we going to do with him?" Omar looks at me, his brow furrowed.

"We can't just leave him here. He'll freeze his tiny balls off and he needs food. We're taking him back to the hotel."

"To our room?" Omar raises an eyebrow.

"Yes, why not?"

"Well, for starters, we don't have a litter tray or anything," he protests, though not very convincingly.

"We'll figure it out. We can put him in the bathtub if he needs to go and I can feed him with a spoon or something."

Omar studies me for a moment but he's already given in. There's no way I'm leaving this little one behind, and he knows it. This kitten is coming with us, no matter what.

As we approach the hotel I feel the kitten shift inside my jacket, its little claws occasionally poking through my shirt. The hotel is one of those small, family-run places with a cosy, lived-in vibe. I glance at Omar and he looks back at me, his eyes widening with the realisation of what we're about to do.

"Alright, I'll distract the receptionist," I whisper, glancing down at the kitten, who seems to have settled comfortably against me. "You just get him upstairs without causing a scene."

Omar looks at me, half-amused, half-exasperated. "Bri you know I'm not exactly a cat person, right?"

"Consider it your good deed for the day," I grin, patting his arm. "Just keep him hidden in your jacket. It'll be fine."

"You don't speak Italian," he objects again.

"Exactly. It's going to take her ages to understand me, giving you more time to sneak past her."

Omar sighs, but doesn't argue with me. He carefully unzips his jacket and I gently transfer the kitten into his arms. The little ginger furball meows softly and Omar winces, quickly pulling the zipper up to conceal the stowaway.

"Just try to look natural," I whisper.

"Right, because nothing says natural like having a squirming lump inside your jacket," he mutters, rolling his eyes.

We enter the hotel lobby, and as luck would have it the receptionist is an older woman with a friendly smile. Perfect. I saunter up to the front desk, putting on my best casual, everything's-normal-here face.

"*Buonasera,*" I say brightly, leaning on the counter. "Eh, *scusi... un buon posto... per*, uh, breakfast... *domani*? *Raccomandare*?" *That's not even Italian!* But who cares, as long as it distracts her.

"I speak English," the woman grins. *Shit*, for once I need an Italian speaker but luck doesn't seem to be on my side.

"Could you recommend a good place for breakfast tomorrow? Something with a great view, maybe?"

"*Certo!* Oh, certainly! There's a little café just around the corner—La Terrazza. It has a wonderful view of the valley especially in the morning when the mist is still lifting."

"Sounds perfect," I say, nodding enthusiastically. Out of the corner of my eye I see Omar trying to make his way towards the staircase. He's walking a bit stiffly, like someone who's trying very hard not to draw attention to himself. But the receptionist seems completely absorbed in our conversation.

"And do they serve proper Italian coffee there?" I continue, keeping her attention firmly on me with a ludicrous question. *What else would they serve?*

"Oh, absolutely! The best cappuccino in town," she assures me.

I hear a faint rustling sound behind me, and I turn to see Omar awkwardly adjusting his jacket, trying to muffle a soft meow. My heart skips a beat but I quickly plaster on a smile and turn back to the receptionist, who thankfully hasn't noticed.

"That sounds perfect! I can't wait to try it," I say, hoping my voice doesn't sound as strained as I feel.

Omar finally reaches the stairs and starts to ascend, his movements just a little too deliberate. He would make a shit spy. The kitten lets out another tiny meow and Omar freezes mid-step, his eyes wide with panic.

I clear my throat loudly, catching the receptionist's attention again. "Oh, and one more thing—do you happen to know if there's a good spot for gelato nearby? I'm really craving some."

The receptionist beams, clearly delighted to be of help. "Yes, there's a wonderful gelateria just a few streets away, called Gelato di Nonna. Their pistachio is to die for!"

I sneak a glance at Omar as she speaks. He's reached the top of the stairs and disappears around the corner. I let out a quiet sigh of relief and turn back to the receptionist with a genuine smile.

"Thank you so much! You've been incredibly helpful."

"It's my pleasure, dear. *Buona serata!*"

With that I finally make my way to the staircase, trying not to sprint up the steps in my eagerness to check on Omar and our little rescue.

I find Omar standing in the middle of the room, jacket still zipped up, looking completely bewildered.

"He's still in there?" I ask, a laugh bubbling up despite myself.

"He hasn't moved a muscle," Omar says, his voice a mix of disbelief and something that sounds suspiciously like affection. "I think he's asleep."

"You've clearly got the magic touch," I tease, stepping closer to unzip his jacket.

The kitten slowly peeks out as soon as it's open, blinking sleepily up at us. I gently lift him out and he immediately snuggles against me, his tiny purrs vibrating through my chest.

Omar watches us, his expression softening. "I still don't like cats," he says.

"Sure you don't," I reply, smiling at him. "But you're going to help me take care of him, aren't you?"

Omar sighs but reaches out to scratch the kitten's head. "Fine, what do you need?"

"Maybe you can find a shop that's open where you can buy some kitten formula and a litter tray."

"In this small village?" He's right, not much chance but we'll have to try. The cat can't drink cow milk.

"Please try, Omar," I plead.

He places a kiss on my forehead, grabs the car keys from the table and leaves the room in search of a miracle.

By the time he's back, I've bedded the cat down in the bathtub on top of a towel. I used another towel to cover him and give him some warmth.

"Did you find a shop?" I ask excitedly when I see all the bags in his hands.

"No, Maria had some."

"Who the fuck is Maria?" I ask confused.

"Well Snaily," he gives me a quick peck on the lips, "She's the receptionist's cousin's husband's sister and the local vet."

"You told the receptionist," I gasp.

"It's alright Mata Hari, no need for the MI6 routine anymore. She was absolutely fine with it and she helped me get some formula for the cat, a syringe to feed him with, and a litter tray." He holds up all the bags.

I pull him close and kiss him deeply. "Thank you!"

"Sure," he replies with a happy smile.

Omar heads back down to the get the formula warmed up whilst I set up a litter tray for the furball. He keeps meowing at me loudly. I guess he's hungry.

"Here you go," Omar holds out a cup of warmed goodness for the little kitten. I get him to fill the syringe whilst I grab the cat and cuddle him to me.

"We should give him a name," I suggest whilst feeding him.

"I don't know—"

"Come on. He loves you so maybe we'll name him after you."

"No way." Omar shakes his head, grabbing a bottle of water from the minibar.

"Well, let's see." I hold out the syringe and Omar refills it so I can give the cat a little more. "He's orange, and it's autumn... pumpkin. What's pumpkin in Italian?" *Please let it be something nice, please!*

"*Zucca*," Omar replies.

"*Zucca*," I repeat.

"Say it softer, it's pronounced more like it's written with an s at the beginning and only one c." My Italian still stinks even after the time we've spent here but I try it again and Omar claps.

"*Perfetto*!"

"Is that your name little one? Zucca?" I pad his head as he's licking the formula from around his mouth and just blinks at me.

I take Zucca and carry him to the bathroom to show him the litter tray. Not sure if he'll get what it is, but cats have an instinct to bury their poop and pee. I build him a small nest of blankets on the floor next to me and then get myself ready for bed.

"What are we going to do with him tomorrow when we move on?" I'm sad to say goodbye to the little furball already, but taking him with us just won't work.

"Maria offered to take him. She has a few cats already," Omar tries to reassure me.

"Okay," I sniffle and curl up in his arms. Just as I'm about to switch off the light there's a tug on the sheet. Zucca is trying to jump onto the bed but it's too high for him, so I gently grab him and lift him up. He stumbles around between me and Omar before crawling on top of him and snuggling up against his chest.

"See, he likes you," I cheer.

"Don't get why. You're the cat lady," he grumbles.

"Maybe you're a cat man."

"I am *not* a cat man!"

"Zucca likes you," I grin. Omar sighs but doesn't reply and carefully picks the ginger furball up, pulls me into his arms and places the cat in front of me so Zucca can snuggle up against my belly. That's how we fall asleep. The three of us.

The first rays of sunshine hit me directly in the face and wake me up. We forgot to close the curtains last night. I turn and find Omar sleeping on his front with Zucca curled up between his shoulder blade and his neck. The cat clearly loves Omar. They look so cute that I just have to take a photo.

Leaving Zucca behind breaks my heart but Omar's right. What would we do with him on the long car journeys? And he'd need all sorts of vaccinations before we could take him across any borders.

When I come out of the bathroom Omar is sitting up with Zucca on his lap. He's stroking the little ginger between his ears and the furball is purring loudly.

"Fight it as much as you want. He's your feline friend now," I giggle.

"Apparently," Omar replies. He tries to be grumpy about it but I see a little smile tugging on the corners of his mouth.

"Come here," he holds out his arm for me.

"No, Mister. As much as I'd love to cuddle with the two of you we have to get going, chop chop, *Snaily*!"

He sighs but knows I'm right. In all honesty, I just want to get the goodbye with Zucca over as soon as possible. Rip off the plaster and move on. The longer we have him the more I'll fall in love with him and I'm already close to crying.

Two hours later, after a tearful goodbye from me and a stern goodbye from Omar—although I think he was just trying to hide his emotions—we're on the way to San Marino.

We are both lost in thought as we drive through the countryside. I feel guilty for leaving Zucca behind. Maria seemed nice and there's a lot of space and other cats for him to play with but I would have preferred to keep him. I'm pretty sure Bella would have gone mental though. She doesn't like to share attention with anyone.

"You're sad you couldn't keep him, aren't you?" Omar asks.

"A little. Is that crazy?"

"No," is the only reply I get.

"He has a good home. I'm just a sucker for cats."

"Ha, don't I know it," Omar laughs.

An hour later we turn onto the winding road that takes us to San Marino. This place is something else—San Marino isn't part of Italy but is its own little city state. It's perched on the steep slopes of a hill, with the city walls, towers, and a castle hugging the ridge. The roads here are very narrow and some are too tight for cars. We've been told to park in a lower car park and take a lift up to the town centre.

Our hotel is right in the heart of it all and just a minute's walk from Piazza della Libertà. It's a lovely family-run spot, they make us feel right at home from the moment we arrive.

"Have a look at this," Omar waves me over. I open the window and the view takes my breath away: the rooftops of San Marino stretch out below our window before the slopes drop steeply into the valley, with green meadows and other hilltop villages in the distance. It's like something out of a fairy tale.

We spend the rest of the day exploring the quaint Christmas market. With December just around the corner, the streets are decked out in twinkling lights and festive decorations. There's a real Christmas buzz in the air which makes everything feel extra special.

"I'll take you up to the ridge tomorrow," Omar mumbles as he places a kiss on my neck.

"More hiking," I groan. "These Italian villages all seem to be on impossible steep hills. I'm starting to feel like a mountain goat."

"Snaily, you'll be fine," he laughs and drags me back to our hotel. *Goody, make out time!*

♥

It was worth the climb because the view from the city wall on top of the ridge is amazing. I can see all the way to the coast and the small town of Rimini.

We follow the footpath past the Prima Torre and Seconda Torre. The further we walk, the less people we see. The footpath gets narrower as we approach the Terza Torre; the third tower.

"I can't believe we're close to the end of the trip," I suddenly say.

"Five days doesn't sound long."

"Five days," I repeat. It sounds like nothing. Almost time to return to my life. Start studying. A life shared only with Bella and the occasional visit from Ruthie and Christopher. I shouldn't be ungrateful. There are also the girls. And... I'm just grumpy because I don't want this to end.

I don't say any of that out loud. He doesn't need to be part of my pity party. He'll think I'm pressuring him but I haven't forgotten what our deal was. Doesn't mean I'm not sad that our time is running out though.

The Terza Torre is a lonely tower with not much to see, and even the view is obscured by bushes and trees. Just as I'm about to complain about it Omar pushes me gently against the rough stone wall of the tower. He cages me between his arms and the wall of the tower and starts to kiss me. At first it's a harmless little kiss but it turns passionate very quickly.

"I can't get enough of you," he whispers, his voice laced with desire. "Let me show you just how much I want you."

I wrap my arms around his neck, deepening the kiss. The heat of our bodies combined with the warmth of the sun creates an intoxicating sensation.

Omar's hands roam over my back, giving me goosebumps. I let out a soft moan, overwhelmed by the desire coursing through me.

He breaks the kiss and slides his hot lips along my jawline and down my neck. I tilt my head back, basking in the pleasure of his touch.

His hands move lower, cupping my ass and pulling me closer to him. I can feel how hard he is against me and it fuels my need.

I run my fingers through his short black hair as he nips at the sensitive skin of my collarbone. My body feels like it's on fire, every nerve ending alive with anticipation.

Omar's hand slips beneath the waistband of my yoga pants and finds its way between my thighs. I gasp as his fingers brush against the wet fabric of my knickers.

He looks into my eyes for permission, and I nod eagerly. He pulls aside the fabric with one smooth motion and plunges two fingers inside me.

A low moan escapes from deep within me as he begins to move his fingers in slow circles. I lean back against the tower as all my senses go in overdrive.

Omar kisses me hungrily as he finger-fucks me with increasing intensity. My legs tremble beneath me, threatening to give way at any moment.

I'm lost in a haze of ecstasy and world around me fades into the background. The only thing that matters is the feel of his fingers inside me, bringing me closer and closer to the edge.

I sense my climax building like a storm gathering on the horizon. Omar's thumb brushes against my clit which sends sparks of pleasure through my body.

I stifle a cry by pressing my mouth into his shoulder as I finally tip over that edge, my orgasm crashing over me. I cling to Omar as my body shakes with the force of it.

He holds me tight as I ride out the waves of pleasure, his fingers still moving gently inside me. When I finally come back down to earth, he kisses me softly.

"God, you're incredible," he whispers. "I love making you come."

I love it too, too much to be honest. The intimacy between us is so intoxicating, it leaves me feeling drunk. It's like a drug and I'm not sure if any other man, or my hands for that matter, will ever be enough after having had Omar.

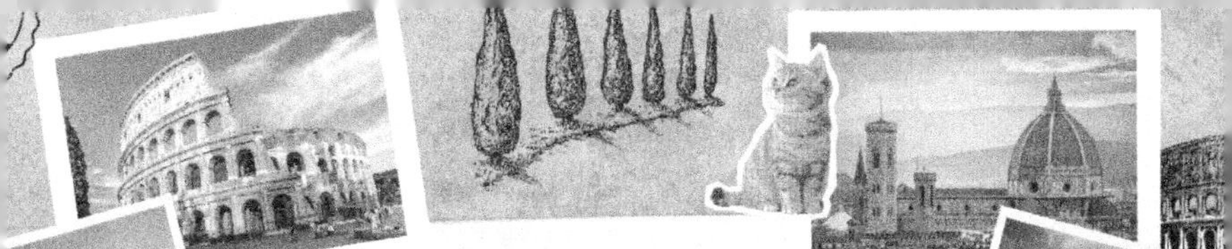

Twenty-Two

Il desiderio

The Wish

Omar

TWENTY KILOMETRES TO VERONA. We've made good progress today, we didn't stop much and instead just ploughed on. It was a quiet drive aside from the music coming from the radio. It's like we're both stuck in our own heads. Something is going on in Bri's mind and I wish I knew what it is.

"So, what are your plans after this trip?" Bri breaks the silence. I give her a glance before focusing on the road.

"I meant to mention it. I received an email this morning offering me a job at our embassy in Jordan. Apparently they're happy to keep the job for me until I get confirmation from my uni."

"Oh, wow. Congratulations! A government job after all," Bri replies. She doesn't sound too enthusiastic but neither did I. My concerns about working for the government remain and I'm wondering if it's the right step for me. But it's a job. It's something to build my future on.

"Yeah, well. Might be fate telling me to go for it," I shrug.

"Jordan," Bri mumbles but doesn't say anything else.

"Yeah, at least I'll be close enough to visit some of my family in Lebanon." I shrug.

"I've never been," she says without looking at me. I almost ask her to come and visit but what would the point be of that?

"What about you?" I ask instead.

"Me? Well, I've my son's wedding and then Christmas and then I'm going to study, I guess." She pops another sweet in her mouth. "You know what's funny, Omar? When I was younger, I thought by the time I'm forty I'd have it all sorted out. I'd live the life of a housewife and mother and... wait for death, I guess. It never crossed my mind how boring that sounds."

"When I was in my early twenties, all I heard from my mum, from my brother was that I should marry. I should have children now so I'm young when they're grown and can enjoy life. But the way you travel when you're in your twenties is completely different from how you travel in your forties. At least it is for me. Slumming it with a backpack in a youth hostel was an adventure back then but I wouldn't want to do that now. It's not that I'm less adventurous, I still like adventure but I want to be able to enjoy it and that means spending a bit more money to make it worth my while. I'm glad I travelled when I was younger and I never really thought I was missing out, but it would be a lie to say it never feels lonely to be the only single person in a room of married people."

She gives my hand a quick squeeze before falling silent again.

There we are two lonely people who weren't quite so lonely for the last few weeks.

I'm standing next to Bri at the bus stop, bundled up in my jacket and beanie, trying to fight off the autumn chill. We're in the north of Italy, close to the Alps, and even though the sun's out, the wind seeps through your clothes if you're not careful. Still, the sky's clear, the kind of crisp blue that makes everything look sharper, and Verona feels like something out of a storybook. Cobbled streets, stone buildings, a city practically dripping with history. We decided to spend a few hours here before travelling to our next destination.

"This better be worth it," I say, glancing at the bus timetable with a raised eyebrow. "We've only got a few hours here and you're dragging me to Juliet's balcony, of all places?"

Bri nudges me with her elbow. "Oh, don't act like you're not curious. You love a bit of drama and romance. Plus, it's iconic! You can't come to Verona and skip Juliet's balcony."

"Sure, nothing like staring at a bit of stone where a fictional girl supposedly stood. Very romantic."

"Well, when you put it that way. But it's not about the balcony, it's about the atmosphere, the love stories."

I smirk. “Are you a romantic, Snaily?”

The bus rumbles up to the stop and we climb aboard, heading straight for the top deck. It’s an open air bus and the wind cuts through us as we sit down, but the views of the city are worth it. Verona spreads out like a postcard: piazzas, churches, old bridges, all soaked in centuries of history.

I relax back in my seat, one arm draped casually over the backrest. Though I was moaning about doing this earlier, the truth is, I’ll take her to any sight she wants to see, as long as it means I get another opportunity to hang out with her. It feels like just yesterday when we said we still had nine days left, and now we’re on our way to Padua, where we’ll stay for two nights before heading to Salzburg for a brief stopover, and then we’re heading home. It’s going too fast and I can’t shake the feeling that I’m not ready for it to end.

“Hey,” I say, pulling Bri from her thoughts. “You alright? You’ve gone a bit quiet.”

She blinks and gives me a quick smile. “Yeah, sorry. Just taking it all in. Verona’s gorgeous, isn’t it?”

“Has there been any part of this trip you haven’t liked?”

She doesn’t hesitate. “Saying goodbye to Zucca.”

I don’t reply to that. Instead, I lean over and press a soft kiss to her forehead. We sit in comfortable silence for the rest of the ride as the bus weaves through the city, until finally we spot the sign for Juliet’s balcony. I catch a glimpse of Bri’s excitement as the bus stops and even though I’ve been mocking this whole visit, I have to admit that the excitement is contagious.

"Alright," I say, following her through a narrow archway as we join a small crowd. "Let's see what all the fuss is about."

Really the whole thing isn't particularly impressive. It's a tiny stone ledge tucked into the side of an old building, covered in ivy and buzzing with tourists. Some people are taking selfies, others are leaving notes on the wall, sticking them in every available crack between the bricks. It's cheesy but I guess there's a certain charm to it.

Bri's got a look in her eyes like she's been waiting her whole life to see this. I snap a few photos of her, and then we wander over to the wall where people have scribbled their messages. I'm actually enjoying this more than I expected. Bri even manages to convince me to rub Juliet's statue, specifically the right breast because apparently it brings luck in love. I'm not looking for love but a bit of luck never hurt anyone.

Bri looks up at me with a mischievous smile. "Now, where do I leave my note?"

I raise an eyebrow, curious. "You're actually leaving one? What's it going to say? 'Dear Juliet, please tell Omar to stop moaning about sightseeing trips'?"

She laughs, that carefree sound I love. "That's not what these letters are for, and you'll never know."

She pulls out a piece of paper, quickly writes something on it and tucks it into a little gap in the wall. I watch her, intrigued, but when she turns around she's got that same smirk on her face.

"Alright," I say, stepping closer. "What did you write?"

"Nope," she grins. "It's a secret."

I narrow my eyes, playfully. "Come on, Bri. What was it?"

"You'll have to ask Juliet yourself," she teases.

I sigh dramatically. "Great. I'm going to be wondering all day."

"Good," she says. "Keeps things interesting. Now excuse me." She points at the gift shop and leaves me standing alone. She loves a gift shop and the amount of little trinkets in the Beast is laughable. She even got me a little snow globe of a Roman soldier after my moment of jealousy.

My eyes drift to where Bri put her note. I shouldn't, but if I do I'll have to be quick. My eyes fall back to the shop and there's no sign of her. I take a step closer. I can see her note stuck between the bricks. It's calling for me. I take a deep breath and turn away from it.

It wouldn't be right, even though I'm dying to know what she asked Juliet for. Maybe she'll tell me one day, and if she doesn't, I guess it just wasn't meant for me to know.

The sky is darkening as we head back to the bus stop and there's a real bite in the air. I slide my arm around Bri's shoulders, pulling her close as we walk.

"Hey," I say, breaking the comfortable silence between us. "If I had to pick a balcony to climb for someone, it'd probably be this one."

She laughs but there's a little tension in her voice that wasn't there before. "Good to know. But maybe hold off on the climbing for now. I don't fancy having to call an ambulance when you inevitably fall."

I grin. "Your trust in my climbing abilities is encouraging. But I'd fall gracefully, obviously."

"Obviously," she says, rolling her eyes.

We hop back on the bus and as we sit down she leans her head on my shoulder, the cold air nipping at our faces. The city passes by in a blur of lights and shadows, and I close my eyes for a moment to listen to the gentle voice of the audio guide.

I know time's running out. I know this trip will end soon. But for now, I'm just going to enjoy every last second of it.

It's our first full morning in Padua and I've got to admit that this city's got a certain vibe. It's the first time I've been here and I am glad we stopped. It's not as in-your-face as Rome or as picture-perfect as Verona, but it feels more lived in, like it's got its own rhythm. The streets are quieter and the buildings have a faded charm, like they've seen everything and are in no rush to impress anyone. I get it. I feel a bit like that sometimes.

Bri and I stroll through the main square, Piazza delle Erbe, looking at the market stalls and old stone buildings. Bri's ahead of me with her hands stuffed in her pockets, her hair bouncing slightly as she walks, humming a tune I can't quite place. She's been in a good mood all morning and it's been rubbing off on me.

Bri insists on finding a little café with outdoor seating, which seems ridiculous considering it's bloody cold.

"It's the atmosphere, Omar," she says, like that's supposed to make me feel warmer. But she's already ordering croissants and cappuccinos so I just grin and go along with it.

I sit back in the chair and pull my beanie lower, watching Bri as she collects our order from the counter. She's all wrapped up in a big coat but still looking so sexy. It might be because I know what she's hiding under the coat. She let me explore her beautiful body again last night and I plan to do the same once more today.

Bri brings the tray over with a smile and sets it down between us.

"Look at that," she says, breaking her croissant in half. "This is living."

I teasingly raise an eyebrow. "Cold croissants in November? That's your idea of luxury?"

She rolls her eyes at me but there's a smile tugging at her lips. "You're impossible."

We sit there for a bit, enjoying the peace. The market's bustling in the background, but at our little café table it feels like the world's slowing down just for us. Bri's got a way of making everything feel... lighter. Less complicated.

Suddenly a little bird hops onto the pavement near us, head cocked to the side like it's sussing us out. It hops closer, clearly eyeing up Bri's croissant.

"How sweet," Bri whispers, her eyes lighting up. "A little visitor."

She tears off a piece of her croissant and holds it out, crouching down a bit with her hand extended. I watch, amused, fully expecting the bird to scarper the second it gets close. But no, the little thing hops right up and pecks at the croissant, nibbling from her hand.

Bri beams at me. "Can you believe this?"

I lean back, crossing my arms, trying to suppress a smile. "You've gone full Disney princess."

"Shut up," she laughs, still feeding the bird. "This is adorable."

She's down there focused on the tiny bird with cheeks flushed from the cold, and for a moment I catch myself thinking how... nice this is. Bri being Bri, making the world seem softer. I never really thought I'd enjoy something like this, but here I am watching a bird eat from her hand, and it's one of the best moments I've had in ages.

She looks up at me, catching me staring. "What?"

"Nothing," I say quickly, looking away. But inside, my brain's running wild. *What the hell are you doing, mate?* I don't do relationships. I've made that clear. They're messy, complicated, and someone always gets hurt. I meant it when I gave Bri that explanation and I'm not about to change my mind. But here's the thing—I can almost see it with Bri. Like a version of me that's maybe... softened a bit, ready to let someone in.

I shake the thought away. *Nope, that's not me.* Relationships are for people who don't mind getting hurt, and I'm happy with my life. I have a new job waiting for me that will take me away from England. Besides, we both know the deal.

Bri's still focused on the bird, her face lit up like she's just found a new favourite thing to do. The bird eventually hops off, satisfied, and Bri sits back down with a grin.

"That was amazing," she says, finishing the last bit of her croissant. "You missed your chance to feed it, by the way."

I shrug. "It preferred you anyway," I wink.

I'm still trying to shake off the weird thoughts in my head. How can I suddenly start thinking about relationships? What's wrong with me? I've gone the last twenty years without one. Why am I suddenly considering it? I glance at Bri again and know the answer is sitting in front of me.

We finish up at the café and head towards the Basilica of Saint Anthony, one of Padua's big landmarks. It's domes and towers are impressive and Bri's already pulling out her phone to take photos.

"Omar," she says suddenly, snapping me out of my thoughts. "Look at this."

I turn to see her pointing at a street artist, one of those guys who does caricatures. She's grinning at me and I already know what's coming.

"No," I say, shaking my head.

"Yes," she insists. "It'll be fun! Come on, we need a caricature of us."

"I don't want to see my head five times its normal size."

"That's the point! It'll be hilarious."

I groan but she's already dragging me towards the artist so I give in. Before I know it we're sitting on a bench while the guy's sketching away, his hand flying over the paper. Bri's giggling next to me, probably already imagining how ridiculous we're going to look.

I glance over at her again. She's so full of life and it's like every time I think I've got her figured out she surprises me. It's been a long time since someone surprised me.

After a few minutes the artist holds up the finished product with a flourish and it's exactly as bad as I imagined. My head is enormous, my hair's sticking up in all directions, and Bri's grinning with huge, exaggerated eyes. We look completely ridiculous and Bri's laughing so hard she's clutching her stomach.

"Oh my god," she gasps. "We're framing this."

"No, we're burning it."

She wipes away a tear, still laughing. "It's brilliant."

I shake my head, grinning despite myself. "You're mad."

She tucks the caricature under her arm and leans into me, still smiling. "You love it." She presses a warm kiss to my mouth before paying the artist.

Maybe, just maybe, she's right. I'm realising I love this. The ridiculous moments, the unexpected fun, the way she can make something as simple as feeding a bird or getting a stupid drawing feel like the best part of the day.

Twenty-Three

Das Lied

The Song

Omar

WE HAVE ONE LAST cappuccino and croissant at the border before crossing into Austria. Our adventure is nearly over, and we just have two nights in Salzburg before the drive back to England. I catch myself wondering if I should suggest giving us dating a real shot but I remember that relationships in the real world aren't like the magic we've had on this trip. *Why risk spoiling something so perfect?* Besides, I'm heading to Jordan soon so what's the point? The last few days have been an emotional rollercoaster, that's for sure.

We drive through the Alps towards Salzburg. I've been there a few times when I lived in Tyrol—day trips, ski runs, that sort of thing. As we get closer I catch my first glimpse of the fortress sitting proudly on the hill in the middle of the city. I follow the sat nav and take the Salzburg South exit. We roll up to the first traffic light, and when it turns green I press the accelerator... but nothing happens. The car stutters and then dies.

"Oh, fuck!"

"What's happening?"

"I think the fault's back." The car sits lifeless. I try the ignition again but there's still nothing. Drivers behind us start honking, angrily swerving around us and I put on the hazard lights to let them know we're stuck.

"What are we going to do?" Bri asks, her voice laced with worry.

"You're going to have to push," I say, glancing over at her.

"Me?"

"Unless you want to drive the car. Someone's got to steer. I'll help get it rolling and we can push it over there." I nod towards a small car park just off to our right.

She gives me a look that's half-concerned, half-amused but climbs out of the car. We've faced all sorts of challenges on this trip so what's one more?

"Right. Just say when." I hop out and join her for the first push. There's a little driveway leading down into a car park and if we can just get the car over that small bump the slope should do the rest, and we'll be able to park it safely until we can get help.

"One... two... three... push!" Bri gives it everything she's got and I hear her groan with the effort. I push too, and we just manage to get the car over the little hump at the entrance to the shallow ramp leading down into the car park. I feel the car start to roll, so I quickly jump back into the driver's seat as it glides down into the car park. I steer to the left, letting it roll as far as it'll go before it comes to a stop.

Bri walks over, pulling her beanie lower and zipping up her jacket against the cold. There's a slight flush in her cheeks, a mix of the chilly air and the effort she just put in. I give her a grateful smile as she reaches the car, her breath puffing out in little clouds. "It's fucking freezing," she says, her nose already turning red from the cold wind.

"Okay, let me go and speak with the receptionist of that company," I suggest. We're in the car park belonging to a company called J. Kraus & Söhne. Bri nods and gets back into the car to shelter from the wind.

The warmth of the entrance hall of the building feels like a relief.

"*Grüss Gott*," the young woman on reception greets me. I remember enough German to explain the situation and she's more than happy to let me leave the car here until I can find a mechanic. Luckily Bri signed up with the AA after our issues in Castiglioncello so this time round getting the car fixed should be easier. The receptionist takes my phone number just in case and is then kind enough to call us a taxi.

The rest of the afternoon is spent trying to find our hotel, which turns out to be hidden in an obscure little side alley, and dealing with the breakdown cover. We manage to get a tow car booked for the next day to take the car to a garage.

"Do you think they'll fix it tomorrow?" Bri asks. We both know that if they can't she'll have to fly back the day after tomorrow to make it to her son's wedding. That means our trip would be over sooner than we planned, and sooner than I had prepared myself for emotionally. Just by one night but it would feel like a hell a lot more.

“I don’t know,” is the honest truth. I pull her into my arms. And there's a little sob from her.

“I'm sorry,” she whispers. “I'm just sad that this trip is over, I wish it didn’t have to end.”

“Me too.” I should reassure her that she has her family and her cat to look forward to, but I don’t. Instead, we just stand there, holding each other tightly.

“Why don't we go to the Christmas market?” I suggest. “I might be busy tomorrow with the car, and at least this way you've seen the one thing you’ve wanted to see so desperately.”

“That sounds like a fantastic idea,” she grins. I kiss her deeply. Every kiss in the last few days has been deep and passionate. I need to stock up before it’s all over.

We get changed and head down to reception. The receptionist gives us simple directions to the Christmas market; just turn right twice, and we’ll be there. Bri’s buzzing with excitement about a special winter concert happening today so we head out into the crisp evening air, eager to soak it all in.

The city looks like a scene straight from a Christmas card. Twinkling lights strung everywhere cast a warm glow over the cobblestone streets. We turn the corner and find ourselves on the Residenzplatz, one of the main squares surrounding the big cathedral at the heart of the city. The Christmas market is in full swing and buzzing with life, drawing in thousands of tourists.

We stroll through the stalls, admiring the handmade crafts, sampling food, and enjoying a cup of mulled wine each. The sweet, spiced scent fills the air as we make our way towards a stage set up in the far corner where musicians are playing a mix of traditional and modern Christmas tunes. The atmosphere is electric and we're drawn in closer, wanting to be right in the middle of it all.

As we near the stage the crowd thickens and there's an announcement that makes Bri squeal with joy. Helene Fischer! Of all people, it's the one singer whose song Bri hasn't stopped humming ever since she heard it on our journey through France. She grabs my hand, pulling me eagerly into the crowd.

The first song is new to me, probably one of her latest, but it's not long before the familiar beat of Bri's favourite tune starts up. The arrangement is different, slower with an orchestra backing her up—but Bri recognises it instantly. Her eyes light up, and she looks at me with the infectious grin I can never resist.

Another woman joins Helene on stage, adding traditional yodelling to the song before it shifts to the beat we both know so well. I glance at Bri and in that moment, as the music swells around us, everything else fades away. I pull her close and we share a soft, lingering kiss, right there in the middle of the crowd under sparkling lights. It's as if the whole world has been wrapped up in this one perfect moment.

We start swaying to the music and I whisper the words of the lyrics in her ear. This is our song. This song tells our story. This night is just for us.

My lips find hers and we sink into another passionate kiss. A kiss that's almost inappropriate in public. The music creates a bubble around us blocking out everyone else.

It's just us. Just this one night. Our last night together. Breathless in the night.

Twenty-Four

Der Abschied

The Goodbye

Bridget

THE HOTEL ROOM DOOR falls into the lock behind us and Omar presses me against it the moment it's closed

He kisses me and I'm lost. It's just us; the world could end right now and I wouldn't care as long as he keeps kissing me like this.

I wrap my arms around his neck, pulling him closer to me. He cups my face with one hand, the other sliding down to grab at my hip. Our bodies are pressed together so tightly that there's no space between us for air to get through, but I don't need it anyway; he's keeping me alive with just his touch.

And then somehow we're on the bed, our clothes coming off in a frantic rush of hands and lips and desperate need. Every inch of me burns for him like a fire raging out of control that only he can put it out.

His mouth finds mine again and I let him devour me. He moves down my body, taking his time with every inch of skin he touches until I'm arching up off the bed begging for more.

He looks up at me from between my legs and smirks before leaning in to taste me again.

I moan loudly, not caring who hears us anymore as he brings me closer and closer to the edge over and over until finally, mercifully, I lose control completely beneath his touch.

When I come back down from heaven there's a moment where everything is still; time has stopped or maybe it just doesn't exist anymore. And then he's inside me, filling me up in a way that no one else ever has or ever will again. I can feel myself getting lost in him and in the way he makes me feel, and I never want it to end.

I'm so close, so fucking close, and then he's tugging at my hair, pulling my head back to expose my neck. He bites down gently and it's too much.

I come apart around him, shouting his name over and over as he follows me over the edge.

As I lie there in Omar's arms a sense of contentment washes over me. This was exactly where I wanted to be, in this moment with him. Our time together may be coming to an end but I know that this night will stay with me forever.

I turn my head slightly and look up at Omar, taking in every detail—the way his dark hair is tousled from our lovemak—our shag, the sheen of sweat on his brow, the peaceful expression on his face. In that moment, he's more than just a holiday romance; he's my soulmate.

"I'm going to miss you," I whisper, my voice filled with emotion.

Omar's gaze meets mine and I can see the same sentiment reflected in his eyes. "I'm going to miss you too," he says softly. "More than you'll ever know."

We both knew that this was just a temporary escape from reality and when this trip is over we'll part ways and return to our separate lives. But for now, in this moment, we can forget about all of that and just be together.

♥

The small airport is buzzing, mainly with people arriving rather than leaving. Salzburg airport isn't very big, but during ski season it feels too small for all these passengers. Time is ticking. I have half an hour until boarding, but I only need to make my way through security so I can wait a little longer and I want to stay here in Omar's arms as long as I can. We haven't said anything; neither of us wants to talk. I've got my ear pressed against his chest and can hear his heartbeat. It's fast and I wonder if he's as anxious as I am. Every so often he presses his lips against my head and pulls me closer. Neither of us wants to let go.

Turns out the Beast is no more. *Rest in peace, Beast.* Fixing it would cost too much to be worth it but there are a few things that need to be sorted with the car before Omar can leave. He's speaking to a scrap dealer on Monday to get rid of the car. And then he's gonna fly home in a few days.

Tonight's flight was the only one I could get short notice that would get me home in time for Christopher's wedding party. And whether we say goodbye today or tomorrow doesn't change the fact that we have to part. *Remember, you don't believe in happily-ever-afters.* But that thought doesn't make it any easier to say goodbye to Omar.

This past month has been the best of my life, not just because I was in Italy but because he was with me. He made me feel special, like I mattered, and I haven't felt that way in such a long time. My eyes drift back to the screen where the word "boarding" is now flashing next to my flight.

"I have to go," I whisper, my voice catching in my throat. Omar pulls me close one last time, like he doesn't want to let go. He cups my face in his hands and looks into my eyes.

"Thank you," he says, his voice thick with emotion. "Thank you for an amazing time. Thank you for being here. And thank you for making this the best trip of my life."

His words break my heart and fill it with warmth at the same time. We kiss, a lingering goodbye that says everything words can't. As I pull away I know I'll carry this moment with me forever.

I walk towards security and scan my boarding pass. As the barrier opens to let me through I turn one more time. There's pain on Omar's face and he waves, trying to give me a smile. I wave back and then walk toward security. I'm fighting my tears but I eventually manage to get a hold of myself. *Look at it for what it was. It was the best time of your life. Be grateful for that. Be grateful.*

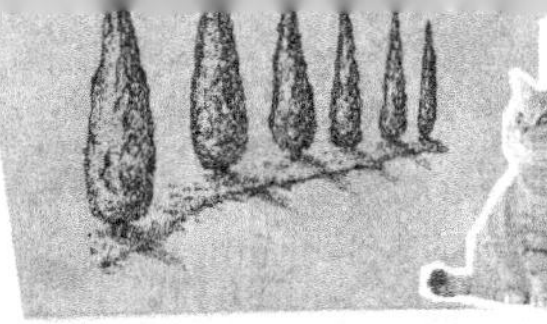

Twenty-Five

The Milf

Bridget

I'M STANDING AT THE bar eyeing the cocktail menu, trying to decide between a gin and tonic or something a bit more festive when I feel a presence next to me. It's Christopher's friend Sam. He has been friends with my son since primary school. Now Sam's all grown up, tall and broad-shouldered with the sort of charming smile that screams trouble.

"Bri," Sam says, leaning a little too close, "you're looking stunning tonight."

I blink. Bri? Since when has he called me by my first name? And "stunning"? I look around, half expecting to see someone else standing behind me, but no, it's definitely me he's talking to. I raise an eyebrow. "You alright, Sam? Had a bit too much champagne, have we?"

He grins, not at all put off. "Nah, just being honest. You're the hottest mum at the party, easily."

I snort, trying not to laugh out loud. Hottest mum? This is my son's wedding party and Sam's flirting with me like we're at a dodgy nightclub.

"Well thanks for the compliment," I say, trying to keep it light, "but maybe save it for the girls your own age, eh?"

But Sam's not giving up that easily. "Age is just a number Bri. And honestly you don't look a day over thirty. I've always thought you were a bit of a fox, you know."

I choke on my drink and I'm about to tell him to behave when I hear a loud, unmistakable voice from behind us.

"What's going on here then?" My ex-husband William is storming over, his face a picture of barely contained fury. He's got a way of looking completely flustered, like someone just told him his shares have tanked. His eyes flick between me and Sam and I can practically see steam coming out of his ears.

"Oh for god's sake," I mutter under my breath. The last thing I need right now is William throwing a tantrum at our son's wedding party. But of course William being William, he's not going to let this slide.

"Sam, what do you think you're doing?" William demands, his voice a bit too loud for the occasion. People are starting to turn and look and I can see Ruthie cringing in the corner with her drink. "That's Bri! She's—she's—" He splutters, his hands flapping in the air. "She's too old for you!"

"Oh come on William," I say, rolling my eyes. "Don't be ridiculous. He's just having a laugh."

But William's not having any of it. "A laugh? A laugh? This is inappropriate! He's twenty years younger than you Bri!"

To his credit Sam just stands there with a grin, clearly enjoying winding William up. "Mr Johnson, I'm not sure this is any of your concern but Bri and I were just chatting."

"Chatting!" William's practically vibrating with indignation now. "Well, chat somewhere else!"

I grab William by the arm and try to steer him away before he causes a full-blown scene. "Honestly, what the fuck is wrong with you?" I hiss. "Calm down. No one's running off to Vegas to get married. We're at a wedding party, not an episode of EastEnders."

But he's having none of it. "This is outrageous! My ex-wife being hit on by my son's friend? It's indecent! Why did you not stop him?. Aren't you embarrassed to be flirting with someone half your age?" I gasp as anger rises in me but before I can tell him where he can stick his opinion and phony outrage someone else steps between us.

"What's it got to do with you?" Ruthie suddenly asks from next to me.

"Ruthie—"

"No Dad, Christopher and I never got involved in the divorce but I believe when you signed that piece of paper you lost every right to decide who mum can date and who she can't. And if a young guy thinks she's a MILF it's got nothing to do with you." I give Ruthie a smile.

"MILF. What's a MILF?"

"William, you're such a clueless prude," I laugh as I walk away from him. I grab a glass of water from the nearest table and head outside. I need some fresh air.

I'm still reeling from the fact that William acts like no one could possibly fancy me, just because he lost every interest in me. That's when Ruthie suddenly appears next to me.

"Can we talk?" she asks.

"Oh, no," I sigh, already bracing myself. "What now? If this is about your father losing his mind over Sam?"

"No it's not about Dad." Ruthie glances around to make sure no one's listening and pulls me a little further into the garden. "I just wanted to check if you're okay?"

"I am darling, don't worry." William can be a pain in the arse but I don't let him piss on my fun anymore.

"It's just that you looked sad in there." She gives me a small hug.

"I'm fine, trust me." I take a sip from my glass. Why is Omar's face invading my thoughts?

"Oh, okay. We haven't had a chance to chat yet. How was your trip?" We take a seat on one of the benches set out for smokers. Neither Ruthie nor I smoke but the heaters are a welcome source of warmth.

"It was a dream," I smile. There he is again.

"What's that smile," she giggles.

"Don't tell your dad but I had a one-night-stand. Your old mum." The only reason I tell her is so I can divert her and my mind from Omar.

"Oh wow. Okay, firstly, you're not old! Secondly, no details please, I'm happy for you to date but I don't want details." She needn't worry, I hadn't planned to tell her about bush-dick and his handcuffs. "And thirdly, why a one-night-stand?"

"Why not?" I throw the question back again.

"I guess maybe you're right. Well, good on you." A shiver runs through her.

"Darling, go inside. I'll come in a minute, I just need a little more quiet time," I give her a hug.

"Okay, oh and mum... stay away from younger guys. You can do much better," she grins before disappearing into the house.

Is five years younger too young?

"Mom, where are my shoes?" *Seriously? I can't believe we're doing this again.* This time it's Christopher. He and his new wife have been staying with me for the last two weeks, and now they're about to fly back to Japan. Suki is lovely and I'm genuinely happy for them both. I really hope it all works out.

"Christopher, you're 24 and married. Surely you can find your own shoes."

"Leave it with me, Bridget," Suki says with a smile and heads off to their room to hunt down the elusive trainers. I lean against the kitchen counter, feeling Bella weave between my legs. Lizzie and Coop were so kind to bring her down from Yorkshire for me. She's finally forgiven me for leaving her for a month; though she had a blast with Smutty she still ignored me for two days before she'd even let me pet her. Now she's back to being my little shadow, mostly because the house has been so busy.

"Hey, Bella bear," I murmur, gently scratching behind her ears. She purrs contentedly before headbutting me. "Oh, you want some food, don't you?" I grab a bowl and squeeze out her favourite pâté. Feeding Bella always reminds me of Zucca. That little kitten was such a sweetheart. I wonder what he's up to now. I wish I could've brought him home with me.

Not a day goes by that I don't think about our trip... the cat, the streets of Florence, the breathtaking sunsets. And, of course, Omar. He texted me when he got back to the UK but we haven't been in touch since. What's the point? I've never been someone who can just be friends with a man they've fallen for. And I did fall for him. I had to finally admit that to myself. I guess that's why it was so hard to come back. But I didn't want to be the one to change the rules of our agreement by asking him to give this a chance. It wouldn't have worked out anyway, with his new job and all.

Christopher and Suki finally manage to gather all their things and hop into a taxi. Christopher gives me a tight hug and I know I won't see him again anytime soon. It's a long and expensive flight from Japan to the UK, and neither of them is exactly rolling in money. I promise to visit them next summer, though. I've set aside some of the money Ruth left me.

The house falls into a heavy silence as the door clicks shut behind them. It's been a whirlwind of activity since I got back and I haven't had much time to think, except for quiet hours at night when I'm alone. But now the silence feels overwhelming.

"You know what we need, Bella?" I ask, looking down at her. "We need a girls' night." Amelia and Ben got back from Yorkshire yesterday, perfect timing for a Christmas get-together. I grab my phone and send a message in our group chat.

Me:

How about a girls' night?

Lizzie:

Hell yes!

Amelia:

I'm in.

Fi:

Just tell me when and where—I'll find a babysitter. Or Ben can watch Max.

Miranda:

I'm so down.

We decide to meet at my place. It's easiest as I'm the only one without a husband or kids. I promise to make my famous burgers and the girls will bring dessert and snacks. I'd ask if they'd like to stay the night, but they all live nearby aside from Lizzie, and Coop will probably hang out with Ben anyway so she can easily get a lift home with him.

As I set my phone down the house already feels a little less empty. A night with the girls is exactly what I need.

The girls are gathered around my coffee table, the room buzzing with their laughter and chatter. It's the perfect kind of chaos to distract me from my own thoughts.

"So tell us, how many Italian stallions did you bed?" Lizzie teases, wiggling her eyebrows.

"None," I say, trying to keep a straight face. It's not entirely a lie because Giovanni doesn't count, it's not like he gave me an orgasm. And Omar? Well, he's not exactly Italian. But let's see if I can get away with half-truths.

"Come on, Bri. I had a feeling you went there on a mission." Lizzie narrows her eyes at me.

"What gave you that idea?"

"You had a glint in your eyes when you talked about the trip," she says.

"Well there was this one guy... bush-dick."

Fi almost spits her drink across the room. "Bush-dick?!" she sputters.

"Yeah," I say, grinning. "His name was Giovanni but because he had a... moderate-sized package but the biggest bush of hair I've ever seen, I kind of gave him a nickname."

Lizzie and Amelia are in hysterics, barely able to breathe through their laughter.

"So, what happened with bush-dick?" Lizzie manages to ask.

"Well, he liked to be tied up."

"Oooh, saucy!" Miranda chimes in.

"He brought his own handcuffs. Wanted me to restrain him and, well, give him a blowie, and then he just... left."

"Rude!" Miranda says, outraged.

"He didn't even offer you a big O in return?" Fi asks, eyes wide.

"Nope. Said he was tired. Thought I'd understand," I shrug.

"Bastard!" Lizzie laughs.

"And there was nobody else?" Amelia asks, still giggling.

"Well," I say, taking a sip of wine, "he did leave a bad taste—literally and figuratively."

Amelia snorts as Miranda and Lizzie clutch each other, tears streaming down their faces from laughing so hard.

"Hang on a second," Lizzie says, her eyes narrowing. "You said no other Italian stallion... Was there someone else?"

I feel my cheeks heat up as all eyes are on me.

"Who?" Amelia presses.

"Oh my God, it was the driver, wasn't it?" Miranda blurts out.

"Omar?" Amelia shouts, wide-eyed.

"I—no, I mean, yes. But we agreed it was just a holiday romance. It's over, done," I say quickly, taking a big bite of burger in a futile attempt to avoid more questions. But of course they won't let me off the hook that easily.

"What exactly happened?" Lizzie demands, leaning in.

I give them the condensed version, leaving out the parts that still make my heart ache. They listen, wide-eyed and silent.

"That's it," I say when I finish.

"Oh my God that is so sweet. You guys are so cute," Fi coos.

"No, no, no," I protest. "It was just a holiday romance. We both agreed."

"Bri, look at me," Lizzie says seriously. "Are you telling me that you didn't develop any feelings for him?"

I stutter, "I—I liked him." Even I don't believe the lie.

"Bri, tell us the truth," Amelia says softly.

"It was just a holiday thing. We agreed," I insist sounding like a broken record.

"Let me ask you a different question," Amelia says. "What happened when you said goodbye to him?"

I'm silent as the memories of that last hug at the airport, that final look, and that kiss come flooding back. I can feel tears welling up in my eyes and one slips down my cheek before I can stop it.

"Oh, Bri," Amelia says, wrapping me in a hug. That's it; I can't hold back the tears anymore.

"I may have fallen for him a tiny bit," I sob. "But that wasn't the plan."

"Have you told him?" Miranda asks gently.

"Of course not!" I object. "We had an agreement. He made it clear he doesn't do relationships."

"Oh my God another one," Lizzie groans. "Did you learn nothing from me or Amelia?"

I look at her, confused.

"I thought Coop wouldn't be interested in me," Lizzie says. "I pretended not to notice that he was pining for me. And Amelia thought Ben could do better."

"And what did we both have in common?" Amelia adds. "We didn't talk to them. You need to tell Omar how you feel."

"What's the worst that could happen?" Lizzie asks. "He could say he doesn't feel the same. But as it stands you don't have him in your life and it's already hurting you. Would it hurt that much more if he said he wasn't interested? And what if he is interested? And he thinks you don't want a relationship because that's what you told him?"

I sniffle, trying to process what they're saying.

"He's got a job offer in Jordan. He's leaving soon," I try as a last protest.

"That's news to me," Amelia looks surprised.

"Look, you need to find out how he feels about you. What do we hate in romance books?" Miranda asks pointedly.

"Miscommunication," the others chorus.

"You need to talk to him, Bri," Lizzie says firmly.

"I'll think about it," I mumble, still unsure.

"No, don't just think about it," Amelia says. "Promise us you'll at least talk to him."

I look at them all, knowing they're right but terrified of what might happen. "Okay," I say finally. "But please let me handle it. I'll do it my way."

They exchange glances but nod. I know they'll stick to their word... for a while at least, but if I take too long they will take matters in their own hands. I would do the same for any of them. Sometimes it sucks to have such amazing friends. You can't get away with shit.

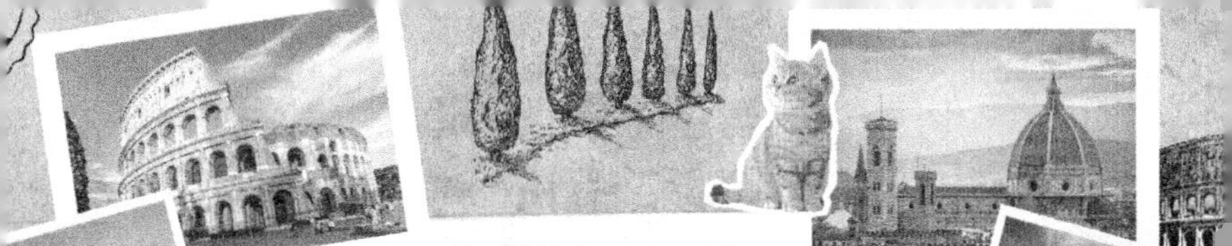

Twenty-Six

The Advice

Omar

"MATE, YOU'VE GOT IT bad."

Russ elbows me in the ribs just as I'm taking a drink of water and I nearly spit it all over the pitch. We've just finished five-a-side and I've been distracted the whole game. Russ can tell, of course.

"You're still thinking about her, aren't you?" he presses, a stupid smirk on his face.

"Who?" *I haven't stopped thinking of her since I made it back a couple of weeks ago.*

"Don't play dumb Omar. Bri. You drop her name into a conversation at every possible moment." He gives me a knowing look, one eyebrow raised.

"I'm not. And I'm not thinking about her," I mutter but the lie tastes sour in my mouth. I tried to tone it down, but every so often I remember something funny she did and it just slips out.

Russ laughs. "Mate, you've been off your game today. Nearly scored an own goal twice. You're miles away and I'd bet anything you're thinking about Bri."

"It was just a fling," I protest, wiping sweat from my forehead, my voice more defensive than I want it to be. "We both agreed. That's all it was."

Russ rolls his eyes. "Yeah, yeah, 'just a fling.' You've said that, like, fifty times. But tell me, how many flings have you been hung up on like this one?"

I don't answer because he knows the answer as well as I do. None.

I stretch my legs out, trying to shake off this conversation as if it were a cramp. "We had fun. It's over. She's doing her thing; I'm doing mine. It wouldn't work."

Russ squints at me, "It wouldn't work? Or you won't let it work?"

I blink, caught off guard. "What's that supposed to mean?"

Russ leans forward, elbows on his knees. "It means you've been saying that relationships aren't for you for years but that's because you're scared. You've convinced yourself they're all doomed so you're not even giving it a chance."

I open my mouth to argue but he cuts me off.

"You're not your dad," Russ says, softer now. "But that's what you're afraid of, isn't it? That you'll somehow turn into him."

I stare at the ground, my pulse picking up. "It's not that simple."

"It is that simple," Russ says, leaning back. "You think all relationships end badly because of what happened with your parents and you're scared you've got his 'cheater gene' or some rubbish like that."

I stay silent, my chest tightening. I've never said those words out loud but Russ has known me long enough to read between the lines.

"So you don't even try," he continues. "You say you don't want a relationship because it's easier to keep things light. But now you've met someone who's thrown you off your game, and you don't know what to do."

I scoff, shaking my head, but his words hit home. "It's not that deep. Bri and I agreed it wouldn't become more than a fling."

"And you believe that?"

"She said it."

Russ raises an eyebrow. "Yeah but did she mean it? Or was she just following your lead because you're so hung up on thinking every relationship is destined to end in flames?"

I glare at him and his question stings. I think back to the last moments I spent with Bri in Salzburg, the way she hugged me a little tighter than necessary, the way her smile faltered just before she turned to leave. We both said it was just a casual holiday romance with no strings attached. But did she want it to be more? Did I?

Russ doesn't let up. "You know, you've never actually given a relationship a proper go. Not since we were teenagers. And you're not your dad. Just because he messed up doesn't mean you're going to."

"How do you know?" I mutter.

Russ shrugs. "You're right. I don't, except you're worrying about it: you don't want to be like him and that already makes you different from him. You can be better."

I don't say anything, the weight of his words pressing down on me. It's not like I've never thought about it. The fear of becoming like my dad always lurks in the back of my mind, whispering that I'll mess up any relationship I get into. That it's better to avoid it altogether than to risk it.

But Bri... Bri makes me want to risk it.

"You know, it's not just about avoiding being your dad," Russ says after a moment. "You've also got to ask yourself what you want. Because mate, I've never seen you like this. Not even close."

I rub a hand over my face in frustration. "What if it all goes wrong? What if I can't make it work?"

Russ stands up, stretching his arms over his head. "Then it goes wrong but at least you tried. And maybe it won't go wrong. Maybe it works out better than you ever thought it could."

I stay seated and stare down at the pitch, thinking about all the reasons it shouldn't work. There are a thousand reasons not to take the risk, even if I can't think of any right this moment.

Russ shrugs on his jacket and glances at me. "Look, I'm not saying you have to drop everything and declare your love to her but you're not doing yourself any favours by sitting here pretending you don't care. Call her, see what she thinks. You might be surprised."

I stand up, zipping up my hoodie to keep out the cold. "You really think it's that simple?"

Russ grins. "Nothing's simple. But what's the alternative? You, sitting here, thinking about her every day and wondering what might have been? Or you take a chance and actually live a little?"

We start walking towards the car park and I pull out my phone, staring at Bri's number which is still at the top of my contacts list. Russ slaps me on the back as he walks past.

"Don't think about it too much. Just call her. Worst thing she can say is no. And I've seen you deal with worse than that."

I watch him walk off and stand there, phone in hand. Maybe I should call her. Maybe… my fingers hovers over the call button but I close the app and slide the phone in my pocket. Not today.

Twenty-Seven

The Call

Omar

I SINK BACK ONTO my bed and immediately my little ginger furball Zucca, hops onto my lap, tackling my hand which is his favourite game. I've grown to love these moments, where I playfully scruff his tiny face or let him dangle from my arms like a furry acrobat. After my conversation with Russ I felt I had to do something but I just couldn't get myself to call her. I played out at least a thousand scenarios on how the call could go in my head and none of them ended well.

I sent an email to Maria to distract myself. I'm not sure why I checked in on Zucca except that he meant a lot to Bri and maybe I felt that if I took care of him it would be doing something for her. I don't know. I swear an army of therapists could make a living out of sorting my issues.

Maria replied with some photos of Zucca sleeping alone in a corner whilst the other cats were playing together. I knew there and then that I wanted him. I felt an inexplicable need to have him in my life. He's this constant reminder of the time with Bri.

Maria had given him all his vaccinations after we dropped him with her and last week he was finally over the twenty one days the UK government requires between vaccinations and travel. I used some of the money I saved during my trip and bought myself a cheap flight. I booked a train for the return journey because I couldn't face putting Zucca in the cargo hold and there was no flight that would allow me to take him into the cabin.

That tiny ginger furball has me fully under his control already but whatever we do, I always wonder what Bri would do and then it's not difficult to decide to treat him like the little king he is.

Aside from some texts sent when I got back to the UK confirming everything had been sorted, it's been quiet between Bri and me. I've resisted the urge to send pictures of Zucca to her. I don't want her to feel like I'm emotionally blackmailing her into more than what we said this thing would be between us.

My phone buzzes, snapping me out of my thoughts. It's my mum.

"Darling, how are you?"

"Alright, Mum. How's Iceland?" She and Michael spontaneously decided to take a trip over Christmas. Lately all she does is travel and I'm happy for her. She deserves that after everything she sacrificed for me and my brother.

"It's beautiful. We saw the Northern Lights yesterday," she says, her voice full of excitement.

"That's fantastic, Mum."

"What about you? What are you doing for Christmas, darling?"

"I'm not doing much. Not really a Christmas person," I reply, and I can't help but think maybe I could be if the right person were in my life.

"Omar—"

"Don't worry about me Mum. I've got Zucca."

"Oh yes, your cat. I never imagined you'd end up with a cat!" she chuckles.

"If you'd asked me a year ago, I'd have said the same thing," I laugh, scratching Zucca's throat. "But here he is, my little ginger companion."

"So what changed?" she asks in the voice of a mother who can read her children like a book and knows when something is wrong.

"Not sure," I reply. Truth is, I've changed.

"Fine. Keep secrets from your mother. Are you sure you'll be okay alone for Christmas? I know Stu would love to have you over."

"I'm fine, Mum. Really. You have a wonderful time. Say hello to Michael."

"I will darling. And I'll call you on Christmas Day."

"Don't worry about me. I'm doing okay."

"I always worry about you. It's what mothers do."

"Don't stress. Just enjoy yourself." I end the call and find myself staring at my phone. I swipe to the gallery and open a photo I've been looking at a lot lately. It's of me and Bri at the Christmas market concert in Salzburg. We both look so happy.

My heart aches with the memory of our time together. I remember our laughter, the way she made everything seem brighter, and how much I miss her. It's moments like this that remind me just how special the trip was and I can't help wishing for more time together.

My phone beeps.

Stu

Happy Christmas Eve, little brother. Are you sure you don't want to join us for Christmas lunch tomorrow?

Me

Did mum call you?

Stu

Might have ;-) But I'd love to have you here, you know that.

Me

I know. But I'm good, please don't worry. Have a lovely time with the family. Merry Christmas to you all as well!

I know his house will be packed with his in-laws and I'm not sure I'd fit in with a crowd that large this year.

Just as I'm about to put my phone down, it pings again.

Bri

Merry Christmas!

I stare at the message for a moment. After such a long silence her simple words make my heart race. I tell myself not to read too much into a Christmas greeting so I tap out a quick "Merry Christmas!" and, unable to resist, I send her the photo of us at the Christmas market concert.

Her reply comes almost instantly.

Bri

Look how happy we look!

Me

I know, it was a fantastic evening. So, how are you spending your Christmas?

Bri

Oh, just me and Bella. We've got a nice lunch planned for tomorrow.

Me

Just you and the cat?

Bri

Yep, my daughter's staying at her boyfriend's parents' house. So it's just us

Me

Sounds like a peaceful Christmas

No plans on my end either.

Bri

Well, you don't exactly strike me as a Christmas enthusiast.

Me

Who says that?

Bri

Ahem…me

I press the call button before I can second-guess myself. It rings once and she picks up.

"I'd like to tell you that I think you've converted me to a Christmas person," I say.

"Is that so?" Bri replies with a hint of surprise.

"I even have a tiny Christmas tree."

"How tiny are we talking?" she asks.

"About 30 centimetres." I laugh.

"That is the Christmas tree equivalent of bush-dick. So how come you're not spending Christmas with your family?"

"My brother's got his in-laws over so it'll be hectic at his and I didn't think I'd fit in well with that many people."

There's a brief pause and I worry that we're about to end the call.

"What are you cooking for Christmas dinner?" I ask in desperation to keep the conversation going.

"Oh, I've got turkey, pigs in blankets, and Yorkshire pudding," she says proudly.

"Yorkshire pudding for Christmas?"

"Hell yes! Where there are pigs in blankets there must be Yorkshire puddings."

"It does sound delicious," I admit, laughing.

"What about you? Any big plans?" she asks.

"Not really," I say, leaning back on the bed, Zucca curled up on my lap purring softly. "What have you been up to?"

Bri fills me in on her son's wedding and all the drama it involved. It feels like we're picking up right where we left off, as if we'd never been apart.

"I don't think I ever told you so but your husband sounds like a knobhead." She snorts at my remark.

"He kind of is a little. Hence the divorce. But the whole situation was ridiculous, it's ludicrous to think of a younger man finding me attractive."

"I'm younger. And I think you're the most beautiful woman in the world." There's a sharp intake on the other end of the line but she lets the comment go.

"So what about you?" she diverts the focus to me. There's one thing I want to tell her, I want to see how she reacts to my big news.

"I turned down the job in Jordan."

"What? Why?" she asks but it sounds like she's smiling. Hope spreads through me.

"Because... it just wasn't for me."

"Good for you. I like that you follow your heart." She's definitely smiling.

"I have an offer from a charity here in London and I start after Christmas."

"That's amazing." There's genuine happiness in her voice. She asks me more about the job and we end up talking about everything and nothing.

At some point, I glance at my alarm clock and realise it's way past midnight.

"Oh my God Bri, we've been talking for hours. It's two a.m."

"Oops! Merry Christmas then," she says.

"Maybe I should let you get to bed," I suggest, but I can hear the reluctance in my own voice. I don't want to end the call.

"Omar, if you have no plans tomorrow would you like to come over for lunch? I've got plenty of food and it would be nice to have some company."

My heart skips a beat. I want to see her and I think she'd love to cuddle Zucca. "Sure, I'd like that. What time?"

"Come over at noon. Actually come at eleven. We can cook together. You can help with the potatoes."

"Sounds good. I'll be there at eleven."

"Great. Night then!"

"Night."

As I end the call, I can't help but smile.

"Zucca do you want to meet Bri again?" I ask the ginger furball who is currently attacking my hand.

The thought of seeing her, of giving her a hug, making her smile, it feels like someone just gave me the biggest Christmas present ever.

Twenty-Eight

The Right Person

Bridget

I NERVOUSLY TUCK MY hair behind my ear for the fifth time, peering at my reflection in the mirror. Why am I making such a fuss? I've gone for yoga pants to keep things casual but the top I've chosen shows off a bit more cleavage than I intended. I don't want to look like I've made too much effort, but it seems there's no hiding it now.

In the kitchen, the turkey crown sits covered with a big plastic pot to keep Bella's paws away. She paces around being a furry predator, sniffing at the food and making my life difficult. I try to shoo her out of the kitchen but she gives me her best "Puss the cat eyes" look, and of course, I cave.

The clock inches closer to eleven and then the doorbell chimes. Omar is here. I still haven't decided what I'm going to do. I can't exactly tell him how I feel today, of all days. Christmas isn't the time to risk rejection, especially when it could ruin every Christmas to come. Maybe I'm being a bit dramatic, but still.

I head to the front door, trying to keep my nerves in check. I close the living room door so Bella can't make a break for it and pull open the front door. There he is dressed in a beanie and a jacket and grinning like a child on Christmas morning. He's holding a shopping bag in one hand and, to my utter surprise, a cat carrier in the other.

"You have a cat?" I blurt out.

"You might recognise him," Omar says, a hint of mischief in his eyes. He holds up the carrier to reveal Zucca, snoozing peacefully inside.

I gasp. "Is that Zucca? Here? How?"

He shrugs, his smile softening. "I just wanted him with me. He reminds me of the best time of my life."

I feel a tear slip down my cheek. Omar puts the shopping bag down and gently wipes my tears away. "Don't cry," he says softly. "It's good."

We squeeze into the small vestibule between the front door and the living room. Bella, behind the closed door, scratches impatiently. I can tell she's not thrilled about being left out.

I close the front door and open the living room one. Bella immediately zeroes in on Zucca, sniffing his carrier with great curiosity. I carefully let Zucca out of the box and after a moment's hesitation, Bella starts to lick him. Looks like these two are going to get along just fine.

Omar hangs his jacket on a hook by the door and turns to me. He's wearing a grey button-down shirt and jeans, looking effortlessly hot.

"Merry Christmas, Bri."

"Merry Christmas," I reply, just before he pulls me into a tight hug. It's not as intense as the airport farewell but it's close. I inhale deeply, savouring the moment. I've missed him so much.

We stand there, wrapped up in each other, for what feels like both an eternity and a fleeting moment.

"Right, let's get to work," he says, breaking the spell. He follows me into the kitchen.

"What's in there?" I ask, pointing at the shopping bag he's brought.

"Well, only the finest dessert," he says, pulling out a tray of little jars full of creamy Italian goodness.

"Tiramisu! Where did you get those?" I ask amazed.

"There's an Italian place down the road," Omar says, winking. "I know the owner. He owed me a favour so I made him give me six jars yesterday." He places them in the fridge.

"Alright, chef," he says grinning. "What can I do to help?"

After dinner, I lead Omar into the living room. Bella and Zucca are snuggled up together in the little basket by the fireplace, relaxing in the warmth. The twinkling lights around the room give it a cosy, almost romantic vibe. Even though it shouldn't be romantic, I try to remind myself as we plop down on the sofa.

I steal glances at him and all I really want to do is slide over and kiss him. But I can't.

"Bri, can I ask you something?" he says, breaking the silence.

"Sure, what's up?"

"Do you... do you ever think about our trip?" He seems hesitant.

"I think about it all the time," I admit, smiling a little. "Every day, something reminds me of it—something I see, hear, smell. It just was so perfect."

"Yeah," he says, his voice soft. "I wonder if I'm only remembering the good bits but it was just so... right. Even the Beast breaking down led to something beautiful."

We sit in silence for a moment, just staring at the dancing flames in the fireplace.

Go on, say it I try to talk myself into telling him the truth.

"Omar," I whisper before taking a deep breath. "I have to tell you something but you need to promise me that no matter what I say nothing will change between us."

He looks at me, his expression unreadable. "What is it?"

"I think I've fallen in love with you," I blurt out, my heart racing.

He's quiet, his gaze fixed on me, and I brace myself for him to turn me down.

"I know we agreed it was just a holiday fling, and I don't expect anything from you. But in my note, I asked Juliet to give me a sign and here you are. I didn't think we would spend more time together after the trip, but now that we are, it feels like a sign... and I am rambling. I just needed to say it out loud. I love you." Nothing has ever felt more right than saying those three little words.

His eyes soften, and he takes a moment before responding. "Bri, I can't promise that nothing will change after what you've just said."

I hold my breath, waiting for him to finish.

"But I don't want things to stay the same anyway. I want you in my life. I want to kiss you, make love to you, argue with you, and experience life together. I've realised I wasn't interested in a relationship with just any person but I think you might be the right person for me."

My heart skips a beat and I can't quite believe what I'm hearing. I pull him close and kiss him deeply.

"I love you, Omar," I whisper against his lips.

His kiss fills the void that his departure left. I feel whole again, as if the pieces of my heart that were scattered are finally falling back into place. I'm his, and he's mine. We might not be perfect but we're perfect together.

As we pull away I think about Ruth and how she always said everything happens for a reason. If she could see me now, she'd probably say my trip took me exactly where I needed to be—straight to Omar, the love of my life.

Twenty-Nine

Epilogue

The Handcuffs

Omar

WE ROLL INTO VENDEUVRE-SUR-BARSE just before five. The sky has been grey ever since we left Little Hadlow and it made for a stormy crossing to Calais. My family rushes out to greet us the minute the car stops just like last time, and Bri gets a big, affectionate hug from Aurélie.

I lean into Bri and translate, “She’s thrilled to see you again.”

Bri grins back at Aurélie. “And I’m thrilled to see her.”

The evening is the usual chaos. Little kids darting around like they’ve just been given a lifetime’s supply of sweets, and the house alive with chatter, laughter, and the clinking of glasses. Bri fits right back in despite the language barrier, especially with me by her side.

Bri and I decided to escape the Valentine’s madness in London and instead spend a week with my relatives as it is aunt Thérésa’s seventieth birthday tomorrow. Zucca and

Bella are having a sleepover with Smutty, although that black furball was not too pleased when two cats invaded his kingdom.

The birthday party planned for tomorrow has not stopped the family from putting on a big dinner tonight in our honour.

"I'm so full again," Bri moans next to me, gently rubbing her tummy.

"Maybe a workout will help with the digestion," I wink at her and she knows exactly what I'm hinting on. After our Christmas together we started to date in earnest which turned into me spending most evenings at her house. Frankly at the moment I'm paying a lot of rent just to keep my spare clothes safe, but I'm worried that it's too soon to suggest a different living arrangement.

Aurélie insists on showing us to our bedroom after a long day of festive mayhem. She leads us across the courtyard with a steady tap of her cane to a small cottage. The cottage is so quaint and old-fashioned, it feels like stepping back in time even though my cousin Khalid has made sure it has all modern amenities. Aurélie leads us through a small living room to the back of the building overlooking the fields. She pushes open the door to the master bedroom with a flourish, revealing a lovely, inviting space with a big, comfy bed and floral wallpaper.

"This was her and her husband's cottage," I translate for Bri who just nods and looks around. I try to convince Aurélie that she doesn't need to give up her home for us but she assures me that she sleeps in the main building nowadays anyway so that people are around if she needs help.

Aurélie beams as she wishes us goodnight and heads towards the door. Bri moves her suitcase out of the way and it falls over with a crash. The impact dislodges something in the small pocket at the top of the suitcase and the item clatters to the floor with a soft metallic thud.

I look down.

Handcuffs.

Everything freezes for a second. Bri's face turns bright red and I can't help but try to suppress a laugh. Aurélie, looks at me and then at Bri before a big grin exposes her wonky teeth.

"Montre-lui qui est le patron, ma fille!" she giggles.

"She told you to show me who the boss is," I laugh which causes Bri to go even redder than I thought was possible.

Aurélie giggles like a schoolgirl as she hobbles from the room and closes the door behind her.

"What did you have planned for this weekend?" I wink and pick up the handcuffs. I let them dangle from one of my fingers.

"They're bush-dick's," she hisses with embarrassment before snatching them from me and zipping them back up in the little pocket.

"This is so embarrassing," she groans and hides her face in her hands.

"Snaily you've just given Aurélie an amazing story to tell everyone." I pull her into my arms and gently rub her back. "Why do you still have them?"

"I forgot I put them in there in Italy," she shrugs. "I'm sorry."

I smile and kiss her forehead. "Don't be sorry. I think it could be incredibly sexy."

Her cheeks flush pink. "You do?"

I nod. "Definitely."

"Would you like to..." she blushes. We've had some incredible sex but there hasn't been anything crazy. Well aside the outdoor fun we had in San Marino, that is.

"If you're interested, sure," I shrug. She takes the cuffs from the suitcase again and looks at them.

"But what if it's too much?" she asks, worry etched on her face.

I take her hand in mine, giving it a reassuring squeeze. "We'll always communicate, Bri. If anything feels like too much, we'll stop."

A small smile tugs at the corner of her lips as she looks into my eyes, and I see the trust there.

"Then yes," she giggles.

"You want me to tie you up in my crazy family's home and fuck you," I groan. My dick is hard just from thinking about it.

"I... should we wait until we're back home?" She looks at me with big eyes. I lean down and capture her lips with mine in a slow, passionate kiss. Our bodies press against each other, the heat between us building.

"Fuck no," I whisper against her lips.

Her eyes sparkle with desire as she nods eagerly.

"Oh, this is going to be so much fun," I growl. "But first take off your clothes and get on the bed on all fours." I switch on the two small bedside lamps and turn off the main light. The room is immediately cosier and more romantic.

Bri shivers at my words but does as instructed without hesitation. First her shirt drops on the floor, followed by her jeans and underwear. She crawls onto the middle of the bed and presents herself to me so beautifully.

Fuck, she's gorgeous.

My need for her intensifies as I drink in the sight before me—her perfect arse in the air, legs spread displaying glistening folds begging to be touched and tasted.

"How's that feel?" I ask as my fingers trail lightly over her exposed skin.

"S-So good," she moans breathlessly.

"That's just the beginning," I promise.

I kneel behind her, my eyes roaming over her body and taking in every inch of her perfection. The sight of her on all fours is a vision that sends my desire soaring. I can't wait to make love to her.

"You're so beautiful. I could spend hours just admiring your body." My voice is rough, my desire evident in the way I sound. I lean forward, my breath ghosting over her skin, making her shudder. "But I want more than just a look. I want to feel you, taste you, and make you mine."

Bri's breath catches in her throat and she lets out a soft whimper. "I-I want that too," she stammers, her voice a mix of nervousness and anticipation. I tease her with my fingers, running them up and down her thighs before finally pushing two into her warm pussy.

"You're so tight," I murmur, my voice low and intimate. "So ready for me." I add another finger, stretching her further, my fingers gliding easily now as she relaxes around them. "That's it, baby. Open up for me."

Bri's moans fill the room, her body trembling with each thrust of my fingers.

"Oh God, Omar," she pants, her hands gripping the sheets tightly. "I can't believe how much this turns me on. I want more."

"You'll get more, I promise." I remove my fingers. "Now, I want you to lay your head on the pillow and put your hands behind your back.

As she obeys her arse naturally pushes higher. I click the handcuffs in place around each wrist and the sight makes my dick twitch.

“Legs further apart,” I tell her. I support her at the hips as she spreads her legs revealing her glistening folds, her clit swollen and begging for attention. My gaze locks onto her, my desire burning brighter with each passing second.

"So beautiful," I whisper, my voice thick with lust. "I could spend an eternity worshipping this body of yours." I lean forward, my tongue flicking over her sensitive bud. Bri arches her back, a strangled cry escaping her lips.

"Oh fuck, Omar!" she gasps, desperately moving her hands but the cuffs hold her in place. "That feels incredible! Don't stop, please!"

I oblige, my tongue swirling over her clit, my fingers dipping into her wetness and teasing her g-spot. Bri’s moans fill the room, her body writhing beneath me as she rides the waves of pleasure.

"I'm so close," she pants, her voice hoarse. "Omar, I'm gonna—I'm gonna—"

"Come for me baby," I urge, my mouth never leaving her clit. "Let go, surrender to the pleasure."

And with that, Bridget's body tenses, a cry tearing from her throat as she comes undone.

"Fuck that was incredible," she manages, her voice weak. "Having no control, it was..."

I smile against her skin, a sense of satisfaction washing over me. I kiss her softly between her shoulder blades, my fingers trailing down her body, leaving a trail of goose-bumps in their wake. "We're not done."

Bri's eyes sparkle with desire as she turns her head and locks her gaze to mine. "I'm all yours," she whispers, a hint of challenge in her voice. "Do with me as you please."

I smirk. "Oh, I intend to my love. I intend to." I roll on a condom and position myself at her entrance, my cock hard and ready. "Are you ready for me Bri?" I grab onto the link holding the handcuffs and pull, lifting Bri's upper body from the pillow.

She nods, "Please!"

I thrust forward, my cock sliding easily into her wet heat. I pause to let her adjust to the invasion, my hands resting on her hips, holding her in place. "You feel so good," I murmur, my voice thick with desire. "So tight, so hot. Perfect."

A soft moan escapes her lips. "Oh God, yes," she pants.

I begin to move, my thrusts slow and deliberate at first, building in intensity as I keep control of her body. Bridget's moans fill the room and she moves her body in perfect sync with mine.

"Oh fuck yes!" she cries. "Harder, Omar! Faster!"

I oblige, my thrusts becoming more aggressive, my hands gripping her hips tightly as I pound into her.

"I'm gonna come again!" she warns, her voice hoarse. "Oh God, Omar, I can't—I can't hold back!"

"Come for me, baby," I urge, my voice rough with desire. "Let go."

And with that, her body tenses, a cry tearing from her throat as she comes undone once more. Her orgasm rocks her with a powerful wave of ecstasy, her body shaking as she rides it out.

I continue to thrust, my own orgasm building, my cock pulsating inside her. I let go, my body convulsing as I explode. We collapse onto the bed, our bodies spent, our breath coming in ragged gasps. I kiss her softly before freeing her from the handcuffs and getting rid of the condom.

"Well fuck, this is not where I saw this weekend going," I laugh as she curls up in my arms.

"Me neither, but I wouldn't mind if we occasionally revisit these," she nods towards the handcuffs on the bedside table.

"Anytime," I reply and nuzzle against her neck where I place small kisses.

"Shower?" she asks and is about to jump from my arms but I pull her back.

"No, wait just a second."

She looks at me concerned, "What is it?"

"Bri, I... I love you."

"I love you too!" she replies and we melt into another kiss.

"That's good. In which case, how would you feel if I moved in with you?" My heart starts racing. Not sure why I'm nervous. She's hardly going to say no given that we basically live together already. But making it official makes it so... official.

"You want to move in?"

"Well, me and Zucca," I grin.

"Hm, look at us, not long ago we were hardcore relationship deniers, and here we are planning to live together," she giggles.

"I think we've concluded that we were just waiting for the right person to start a relationship with." Pulling her into my arms, I kiss her passionately. "I need to hear it, Snaily."

"Yes, yes of course you can move in," she laughs. "Did you really think I'd say no?"

"I wasn't one hundred percent sure," I grin.

"Omar you crazy man." She shakes her head and is about to kiss me again when I pull away.

"And as we're already moving in with each other I think we should also get married." My heart beats ten times faster and there are a thousand butterflies in my stomach.

"What," Bri breathes and sits up to look into my eyes properly. "We've only been dating for a bit over a year if you count Italy."

I know she's right and I hadn't planned on proposing but now it's said I don't want to take it back.

"Bri, you're my best friend, my lover, my Snaily, my happy place and my travel companion. I'd love to explore the rest of the world with you and have adventures together. But what I want most is to wake up every morning knowing you are my happily-ever-after. Will you please marry me?"

A small tear rolls over her cheek and drops onto her chest where it moistens her nipple. I want to lick it away and taste her again but first I need to hear her answer.

"It's crazy but... I think I... yes, I want you to be my happily-ever-after as well," she finally says.

And just like that we're officially no longer love hermits.

Curious about their adventures? Check out Bri's photo album from the trip:
https://bit.ly/CatLadyRoadTrip

Scan me

Want more Cat Lady stories?

Check out
Valentines Rebellion (Prequel Novella)
&
The Unnatural Habitat of a Cat Lady (Book 1)

Pre-order **The Unhinged Battles of a Cat Lady**!

More from Dani Elias

Fellside Mountain Rescue Series

DO YOU WANT TO meet the guys from the Fellside Mountain Rescue Team? Get the series now:

Blossom with Me

Sing with Me

Paint with Me

Climb with Me

Read with Me

Build with Me

Wrap Up with Me

Ride with Me

Or binge the whole series:

Love at Fellside Vol. 1

Love at Fellside Vol. 2

Cat Ladies Rule The World

You know those "Cat Lady" myths? Forget them! These women are way more than meets the eye. They're not just crazy for cats – there's a whole lot more brewing beneath the surface. Picture this: romance, comedy, and a hint of kink. These books? They're like a rollercoaster ride through the love lives of forty-something ladies who redefine what it means to be a cat lover.

Valentine's Rebellion (Prequel Novella)
The Unnatural Habitat of a Cat Lady
The Unconventional Journey of a Cat Lady
The Unhinged Battles of a Cat Lady

Greenview Manor Tales

Get ready to meet the staff and guests of the **Greenview Manor Hotel**. Explore lost loves, new passions, and hidden romances in these five novellas, brimming with intense emotions and enough suspense to keep you on the edge of your seat.

Fierce Family
Alluring Adventure
Elusive Embrace

Wistful Whispers
Spellbinding Spirit

Aftermath

When aid workers Will, Melanie, and Jon find themselves tangled in an incident with devastating consequences, throwing them into a world of chaos and despair, can their loved ones help them find their way back to life?

Mission
Escape
Rescue

Standalone

Christmas Alibi

Printed in Great Britain
by Amazon

61506084R00157